THE DANGER ZONE

Dave Gustaveson

YWAM Publishing
A Ministry of Youth With A Mission
P.O. Box 55787, Seattle, WA 98155

YWAM Publishing is the publishing ministry of Youth With A Mission. Youth With A Mission (YWAM) is an international missionary organization of Christians from many denominations dedicated to presenting Jesus Christ to this generation. To this end, YWAM has focused its efforts in three main areas: 1) Training and equipping believers for their part in fulfilling the Great Commission (Matthew 28:19). 2) Personal evangelism. 3) Mercy ministry (medical and relief work).

For a free catalog of books and materials write or call:

YWAM Publishing

P.O. Box 55787, Seattle, WA 98155

(425)771-1153 or (800) 922-2143

The Danger Zone

Copyright © 1997 by David Gustaveson

Published by Youth With A Mission Publishing
P.O. Box 55787
Seattle, WA 98155

ISBN 1-57658-002-4

Printed in the United States of America.

To
my loving wife,
Debbie,
for her daily
sacrifice and willingness
to join me in a lifetime
of walking with
Him

Other

REEL KIDS
Adventures

The Missing Video ❖ *Cuba*
Mystery at Smokey Mountain ❖ *Philippines*
The Stolen Necklace ❖ *Kenya*
The Mysterious Case ❖ *Colombia*
The Amazon Stranger ❖ *Brazil*
The Dangerous Voyage ❖ *Haiti*
The Lost Diary ❖ *Turkey*
The Forbidden Road ❖ *China*
The Danger Zone ❖ *Vietnam*

Available at your local Christian bookstore or
YWAM Publishing
1(800) 922-2143

Acknowledgments

Walking a life of faith will ruin you for anything normal. It keeps you on the cutting edge where God shows up. The scriptures teach us that faith is the substance of things hoped for, the evidence of things not seen. The heroes of Hebrews 11 show us the power of faith in action—men and women like David, Deborah, Gideon, and Moses.

The Reel Kids series is designed to challenge even the very youngest to peer beyond daily circumstances with eyes of faith to see the greatness of God and have a daily adventure with Him. Last summer in Atlanta, I had the fun privilege of hanging out with my daughter Jamie and 4500 King's Kids who were living on the edge, trusting God for finances, daily miracles, lost souls, and even nations. They were preparing for an adventure with God that launched them into the world.

I am very grateful for the many people who consistently challenge me to the life of faith. It's easy to retreat to our comfort zones, rather than dare to live on that edge. In my research for this book, I encountered people who overcame obstacles and moved huge mountains by faith.

The church in Vietnam is like that. In the aftermath of a horrible war and daily oppression from

Communism, God's army marches on. His truth marches across the land as people see the evidence of their faith.

A very special thanks to John Dawson for the spark of inspiration for this story. Thanks to Steve Hettick for his amazing insights and years of experience from living in Vietnam. He really has an excellent grasp on the nation.

Also, to Lori Matthias for her love for Vietnam and her help in gathering information. Thanks to Suzanne Howe for her willingness and excitement to read over each detail of the manuscript.

Thanks to Oliver North for writing *One More Mission*. His experience as a Vietnam Vet and a committed believer gave much needed perspective.

Of course, I can't forget the wonderful crew at YWAM Publishing. Thanks to Marit Holmgren for her diligent and insightful editorial comments and fine polishing. Thanks to Frank Ordaz, who once again allowed his paint brush to capture our attention with his amazing cover work.

And thanks to all of you who refuse to retreat to a comfort zone, but rather stick it out with God even in the face of danger.

Table of Contents

understanding glance across the aisle to where Mindy was sitting. He knew the long trip from Los Angeles to Bangkok, Thailand, had taken its toll on all of them.

Mindy's blond ponytail lay undone, begging to be combed. Her pink T-shirt, now crimped and wrinkled, hung partially out of her jean shorts. Sprawled under her seat were her lifeless, pink-laced, white tennis shoes.

The plane's address system crackled. "This is your captain speaking. I apologize for the delay. The jetway jammed against the door makes it impossible to open the door or move the plane. We are unable to restore power to the jetway. We have a skilled crew working to pull it away from the plane manually. As soon as they succeed, we will be towed to a new gate. In the meantime, I apologize for the heat in the cabin."

Jeff raked his hand through his blond, curly hair in frustration. The waiting was getting to him.

"I just want to get to Vietnam," he groaned.

For weeks, The Reel Kids Adventure Club had planned to visit Vietnam, the only place where America had ever lost a war. They were going to film the story of Tom Douglas, a young American visiting the place of his father's death for the first time. In preparation for the trip, the team had researched the horrible war—a war that left 58,000 American soldiers dead and caused great turmoil on American soil in the late 1960s and early '70s.

The club had flown for fifteen hours, beginning at Los Angeles International Airport and entering Asia via Japan. After a two-hour layover, they had boarded a Thai Airline jet to Bangkok. Now they were stuck inside the plane.

Mindy rolled her brown eyes in frustration. Usually her eyes sparkled. Today they were clouded by exhaustion and the smudged lenses of her brown wire-rim glasses.

"It wouldn't be so bad if the air conditioning was working," she said, fanning her flushed face. "But it's so hot. And I'm still hurting from all those shots we got. Typhoid, hepatitis. My arm and backside are still sore."

Jeff nodded to show he understood, then turned to face the seat in front of him. He was too tired to respond anymore. He unconsciously tucked his purple and gold Los Angeles Lakers T-shirt into his black shorts. He knew it was Thursday, June 26, but at this point he felt as if that were the only thing he knew. All he could focus on was arriving in Vietnam to begin their two-week mission. As he studied the dark-featured Asian passengers, he realized how much he loved this part of the world.

Feeling perspiration drip down his face, Jeff put his hand to the tiny air vent. It was blowing only hot air into the cabin. The heat of Asia's summer was invading the cabin by the second. Jeff jumped. A passenger near the back began to shout. Instantly, a flight attendant was at the man's side, calming and soothing him. The sweltering heat wasn't the only thing Jeff could feel in the plane. The tension was tangible.

Jeff was aware of Tom Douglas at his right, talking with the man seated next to the window. Just thinking of filming Tom's story made it worth it to be a member of the Reel Kids Adventure Club and suffer through this hot predicament.

Jeff looked a few rows behind Mindy at Warren Russell, the club's leader, and K.J. Baxter, their cameraman. Warren was head of the Baldwin Heights High School communications department. He had launched the club to take Christian students on outreach trips to other countries and to give them hands-on experience in the communications field.

The trips gave them a chance both to see God in action and to produce videos to inspire other groups to send out their own teams. From experience, club members learned how to do research, write narration scripts, film, and edit the videos. They always borrowed equipment from the school. The principal trusted them and loved hearing the exciting reports of their adventures.

Jeff was the student leader and was in charge of the club's finances. He also did the on-camera work of conducting interviews. He was always excited to share his faith and develop his communications skills at the same time. He had learned a lot from Warren and his own mom and dad about how the two could work together. Both of his parents worked in the field. His father was a TV anchorman for a large Los Angeles station, and his mother was a news correspondent.

What Jeff wanted to do after graduating from college was set up a video production company. At fifteen, he still had lots of time to figure out where he should go to school to build on the skills he was learning on the club's trips. He once told Mindy she should work for him. She said maybe she'd start the company and he could work for her. Mindy, short for Melinda, was the club's ace reporter. She loved to ask questions and did detailed research before the trips. Always on the alert for story possibilities, she took her laptop computer with her everywhere she went. Jeff knew that whatever he and Mindy did after graduating from high school, nothing could replace the experiences they had with the Reel Kids Club.

Desperate for something to do, Jeff reached for the airline magazine in the pouch on the seat in front of him. Of course it was in a language he couldn't read. Seeing the words made him glad that the captain gave the announcements in English first. Next to him, Tom seemed oblivious to the delay, deep in discussion with the man next to him. They were talking about American football. It was a good diversion for Tom, who was only hours away from entering Vietnam. Jeff knew it was going to be tough for Tom once they got there. Tom was only five when his mom broke the horrible news to him of his dad's death in the war. His uncle had asked Warren to film the events of Tom's first visit. He had even paid some of the travel expenses and the cost of the video production.

Jeff felt a tinge of sadness as he looked at Tom now. Tom was a stocky 26-year-old, a little taller than Jeff. Jeff figured he must weigh around two hundred pounds. He had big blue eyes, bushy eyebrows, a squarish jaw, and wavy, dark brown hair. In short, he looked just like the picture Jeff had seen of his father.

Jeff squirmed in his seat, feeling the tension around him grow. He was glad to see his sister lying back in her seat, her eyes closed. Seeing the growing anger on other passengers' faces made him uneasy. He wondered how long the flight attendants could keep control.

A loud banging noise jarred his thoughts.

The address system crackled again. "This is your captain speaking. The crew is still working to free the jetway. I've been flying for over fifteen years and have never seen a jetway stuck this badly. Again, we are sorry for the delay. Let me remind you that the law prohibits you from moving around. For your own safety, we will enforce the law. Please remain seated." The words followed in Thai.

Jeff looked over at Mindy. He was glad when she shot him a half-smile before leaning back in her seat. It was important for the team not to get discouraged. Jeff longed to get off so they could spend a restful evening at their Bangkok hotel before departing for Vietnam Friday morning.

Wishing they were all sitting together, Jeff leaned out in the aisle to check on Warren and K.J. Warren was slumped next to K.J., who was leaning against his armrest on the aisle, his chin in his hand. K.J.'s thick crop of dark hair was sticking up. Warren's hair was so short it always stuck up—it was supposed to.

Jeff loved his leader. His soft brown eyes were friendly and warm. Warren was only an inch taller than Jeff, and they had the same medium build. Jeff guessed his black khaki slacks and green, short-sleeved cotton shirt were wrinkled by now. Without even looking, Jeff knew Warren was wearing brown loafers *without* socks. Even though Warren was in his early thirties, on first glance he looked young enough to be mistaken for one of his students. Adding to the confusion, he had given the group permission to call him by his first name when they were away from school.

K.J. rose slowly from his seat, groaning. Red lines on his face marked where his fingers had been. Jeff and K.J., short for Kyle James, had been best friends since the Caldwells moved to Baldwin Heights. Jeff grinned to see him quiet and subdued, an abnormal scene. His fourteen-year-old friend loved adventure and could be quite impulsive. Jeff both loved and hated K.J.'s wild sense of humor. A tremendous amount of explosive energy was packed into his wiry 5'6" frame. Sometimes that energy helped the team. Other times it got the team in trouble.

"Hey," K.J. said as he moved forward, "you didn't warn us about this. Maybe I should wake Mindy up and see what she thinks."

"Let her alone," Jeff whispered, stealing a glance at Mindy. He knew she was really awake. Mindy in a good mood didn't mind being teased. Mindy hot, tired, and hungry did mind.

K.J. leaned over Jeff's seat. "Maybe I should get my camera out. This would make some great footage for a comedy."

A flight attendant walked quickly down the aisle. "I'm sorry," he said. "The captain has made it very clear that you are all to remain seated until the door opens."

K.J. winked at Jeff and headed back. Jeff grinned. He knew K.J. always kept his trusty Canon Hi-8 camcorder with him, ready to capture any photo opportunity. Though young, K.J. had proven his talent on past projects. He had a steady hand and a good eye.

It was almost seven p.m. Jeff was hungry, and his legs ached. If he were shorter like Mindy or even K.J., he might be able to stretch them. At 5'9" he couldn't. Jeff leaned back in his seat, alarmed. Tom's words were heated now. He and the American were no longer discussing football. The subject had changed to Vietnam. And Tom was getting angry. Really angry.

"You don't know what you're talking about," Tom insisted through clenched teeth.

"What a waste," the man snarled. "That war was a total mistake. Don't waste your time going to Vietnam."

In the close quarters of the plane, Jeff's arm rested against Tom's. He could feel the tenseness of Tom's muscles. He could feel Tom's rage building. Their strained whispers escalated into shouts.

Soon everyone near them was listening to the angry exchange. Jeff didn't know Tom well enough to stop him. Tom's connection to the team was roundabout—Warren was a close friend of his uncle. Most people who traveled with the team were committed Christians and closely screened. Jeff wasn't sure about Tom. But this trip was different. It was an opportunity to film Tom's amazing story, and that couldn't happen without Tom.

Thinking about his own father, Jeff couldn't imagine how horrible it must have been for Tom to lose his dad. He admired Tom's willingness to go to Vietnam, but he feared the volcano of painful emotions that could erupt at any moment.

The conversation grew hotter. Of all the people Tom could have sat next to, Jeff wondered, why was it this American with a bad attitude about the war?

Tom's face was red.

The man smirked. "Why do you think I left the good ol' USA in 1970 and lived in Canada for a while? I didn't want anything to do with that stupid war. They weren't going to draft me. Guys who were smart did like I did. They burned their draft cards and left the country." He laughed in Tom's face.

Tom grew angrier still. Jeff watched him shift in his seat, trying to restrain the flow of adrenaline. From his research, Jeff fully understood why he was upset. Tom was sitting next to a 'draft dodger,' one of sixty thousand Americans who fled the country to avoid having to fight in the controversial war from 1968 to 1975. Of course, not all people who evaded the draft would purposely try to hurt Tom like this man seemed to be doing.

Jeff glanced helplessly at Mindy, who was now sitting up in her seat, very much awake. Looking back, he saw K.J. and Warren leaning forward, their faces creased with frowns. A flight attendant edged closer, obviously scared to confront the angry men.

Their voices grew louder. Jeff had to do something. He gripped Tom's arm and was startled by its explosive tenseness. He pulled hard, determined to get Tom's attention. Tom glanced back, his eyes reddened by exhaustion and rage.

The American scowled. "Stay out of this, kid."

Ignoring him, Jeff peered into Tom's eyes. "Don't let him get to you. He's just looking for trouble. He doesn't have a clue what you've been through."

Tom jerked away from Jeff's grasp, his face flushed. "I could kill this guy. He says the war was a waste. Do you know what that means to me and my...?"

Jeff nodded yes, but he knew he didn't really understand. He sent up a quick prayer, begging for wisdom. The men resumed their bitter exchange. Jeff looked across the aisle at Mindy. His eyes locked with hers, and he knew the whole team was praying.

A flight attendant strode toward them. "What's going on here?" she demanded.

Jeff felt relieved. Someone was taking charge.

"Everything is fine, ma'am," Tom lied.

"Lower your voices then." The attendant shook her head as she walked away.

Jeff felt like shouting, "No, it's not fine!" but he didn't. Maybe their argument really was over. He looked back at Warren. He was obviously trying to decide whether it was necessary for him to disregard the captain's command and get out of his seat. Jeff motioned for him to stay put. He would try one more time.

"Tom," he said softly, "I'm sorry you had to sit next to this guy, but you've got to let it—"

"Look, Jeff," Tom interrupted him. "I'm not going to let this jerk get away with this. Even if the war was a mistake, that's not my dad's fault. It was because of guys like this that the soldiers got no respect. My dad shared the pain of all this in his letters."

Jeff nodded. He didn't know what to say.

"Offer to trade places," Mindy whispered from across the aisle.

"Why don't we trade seats?" Jeff suggested gratefully. "It'll give you a chance to calm down."

Tom ignored Jeff's plea and turned back to the American. "It's guys like you who bring disgrace to America," he hissed.

The man just laughed. Tom clenched his fists and moved in closer. Angry words flew back and forth, this time in low whispers. Jeff needed to signal Warren to come—now.

Just then he felt a sudden jerk, and the plane started to move back. The jetway had been released. Soon they would be at another gate. Away from the man turning Tom into a raging bull. Away from an attack seemingly from hell itself.

Jeff prayed fervently. If the men would hold back their physical anger for just a few minutes, they could get Tom safely off the plane. But to Jeff's horror, Tom raised his clenched fist. His face was red and full of rage, and veins stuck out of his neck.

Chapter 2

Prisoner of War

Without thinking, Jeff grasped Tom's strong, trembling arm, half-aware of Mindy at his side. The frightened American jumped up, inching away from the coming blast of angry flesh. Warren was there instantly, grabbing Tom's other arm to restrain him. Jeff felt adrenaline fill his body, strengthening his grip. His face hardened with determination.

Passengers gasped in disbelief, yelling for help.

The American curled up against the window. "This guy is crazy," he cried. "Get him off me."

Over and over again he cried. In an already tense plane, it was almost too much to bear. Jeff wished he could hide. He wished he could run. But he couldn't let go. Tom was determined to get revenge.

The captain and a flight attendant ran down the aisle. "Stop," the captain commanded, "or I'll have you arrested when we arrive."

Tom wouldn't let go.

"Please, sir," the captain pleaded. "This hasn't been easy for any of us."

That's for sure, Jeff thought, sweat running down his face and his arms aching.

Seconds passed. Finally, Tom relaxed. Jeff and Warren let their arms fall.

"I'm sorry," Tom confessed in a stupor. "I don't know what came over me. This guy really set me off. Get him away from me."

K.J. leaned in. "Tom can have my seat. I'm sitting right there." He pointed a couple of rows back on the opposite side.

The pilot nodded. Tom made his way back to K.J.'s seat, avoiding the stares of puzzled passengers. K.J. climbed into Tom's old seat next to the stunned American.

"Your friend is crazy," the man said shakily. "That war messed up my life from day one. And look at his."

K.J. started to answer him. Jeff reached out and yanked his arm. Immediately, K.J. sat back and turned away.

"Ignore him," Jeff whispered. "Nobody's going to win this argument. It's been fought too many times."

K.J. nodded, his dark eyes wide with all that had happened.

Finally, Jeff felt the thud of the plane coming to a stop. He breathed deeply in relief. He turned around and smiled at Warren. Tom was staring straight ahead, as if in shock. With this kind of a beginning, Jeff wondered what the rest of the trip would be like.

Passengers stood immediately and began to gather their bags from the overhead luggage compartments. Jeff was elbowed in the back as he reached up for his backpack. The crowd pushed to the front of the plane, anxious to get off.

Just as the door opened, the pilot made an announcement. "This is your captain speaking. I have more bad news. It was just discovered that a passenger's purse is missing."

Jeff's head became light. He felt like he was going to faint. Mindy pushed through the crowd to stand by Jeff and K.J.

The pilot spoke sternly. "I'm sorry for the added delay. Starting now, every passenger will be watched very closely. Everyone will be escorted to a holding room to have their bags searched. Again, I'm very sorry."

While he spoke, four security guards came on board. Passengers pressed themselves to the seats as two of the guards squeezed by to the back of the plane. The other two guarded the front.

Jeff couldn't believe it. They hadn't even got to Vietnam, and they were in the middle of another war. A spiritual war. A draining war. At least they could get farther away from Tom's enemy. Jeff's mind flashed back to other trips the club had taken. Their adventures had presented impossible situations, but God had come through. Sometimes He came through at the last minute, but He always came through.

Finally, the security guards began to let people off the plane.

"I should be filming," K.J. whispered. "This is unbelievable."

"I don't think that would be a good idea," Mindy whispered back. "The best thing we can do is fade into the background until we get out of the airport. Tom's going to need a lot of prayer if he's going to make it through this trip."

Jeff knew she was right. All along, his heart had been set on Vietnam, and he still couldn't wait to see the people he had prayed for for months. But now he wished he had understood how hard it would be just to help Tom. Jeff knew there had been many prisoners of war, not just the men who were captured by the enemy, but all the soldiers and all their loved ones. Tom was no exception.

Jeff felt overwhelmed by Tom's loss. "Imagine being five and having your mom explain that your dad was killed in the war—that he's never coming home."

Mindy tucked a strand of damp hair behind her ears. The heat was still suffocating. "And then," she whispered, "imagine growing up and finding out that millions were against the war. No wonder Tom's angry."

K.J. leaned in. "If we're smart, we'll give him space—let him know we care, then give him space."

Mindy looked at K.J. in surprise. Light filled her brown eyes as she realized that K.J. might know something about dealing with pain.

"I just mean that it's tough of him to go through this with all of us watching him," K.J. said, fiddling with his camera bag. "I mean, gosh, we're filming him."

They fell silent as they approached the door. Mindy stepped off the plane first, then K.J. Anticipation filled Jeff as he walked past the guards and into the jetway. They followed a stream of passengers to a large waiting room near the gate. A guard stood by the door. Inside, several more guards were already checking passengers' bags for the missing purse.

Deciding to wait for Tom and Warren, the three of them stood near the entrance. If Jeff knew Warren, he probably waited to be the last ones off the plane so they could apologize to the crew. When they finally came in, Tom stood apart from them. Warren let him be.

"I see you all made it in one piece."

"We did, didn't we?" Mindy said in amazement.

K.J. grinned. "We always make it. It sure is a good thing we planned a night in Bangkok though."

Jeff nodded. "We would have missed our connecting flight for sure. Besides, we're all tired. I could crash in bed right now."

"You're all doing great," Warren assured them. "I couldn't ask for a better team."

K.J. fanned himself. "I just want to lie in front of an air conditioner for the rest of my life."

"That's not a bad idea," Mindy teased. "One big giant ice cube surrounding you. With your camera of course."

"Cold, Mindy," K.J. grunted. "That's really cold."

Everyone laughed, glad to release some tension. The minutes dragged on. The passengers had formed two lines, and the guards were searching the bags one at a time. The thief would have a hard time hiding a purse.

Warren nodded toward K.J.'s camera bag. "We need to be really careful once we get out of here. Just like at home, there are people who make theft a way of life. Some are poor and don't think they have any other choice."

"At times like this," Mindy said, "I wish I was rich so I could help them. Some of them do feel they have to steal to survive. In Vietnam, the yearly income is about three hundred dollars."

Everyone shook their heads in disbelief.

Jeff was relieved to see the man Tom had attacked being searched. That meant he would be leaving soon. He gasped when a security guard pulled a purse from the American's bag. A second guard moved in to handcuff him. The room buzzed with conversation.

"Now I remember," Jeff said. "He left his seat earlier in the flight. And he had his bag with him."

"He must have taken the purse while the woman was sleeping," Mindy said.

"May I have your attention," a security guard called out. "We have found the purse, and an arrest has been made. You are all free to go."

The team members looked at one another in relief. They stepped back to where Tom had been waiting in line.

Tom watched the security guards escort the American out of the room, his expression a mixture of sadness and disgust. "I'm really sorry for what happened," he said at last. "I just lost it in the plane. I should have known what kind of guy he really was, but I...he really brought up a lot of pain." He looked at Warren. "I'm going to need your help to deal with it."

Warren's brown eyes were full of compassion. "We all want to help you. Just let us know when you need space and when you need to talk. And if it helps to know, we won't give up easily. You're doing a brave thing."

"Thanks," Tom said softly. "I appreciate that."

As they walked through Bangkok International Airport, Jeff was surprised at how modern it was. Finally able to relax, he looked around, watching all the people rushing to catch flights or pick up baggage. Parked along the tarmac outside were long lines of 747s painted with the colors of airlines from all over the world. Inside, the new-looking terminal seemed to spread for miles. Soft, calming music played through quality speakers, and all the signs were in Thai and English.

The well-lighted, spick-and-span baggage area was at least two football fields long. When everyone had found their bags, the team headed toward customs. The customs officials were dressed in neatly pressed uniforms. They were all business, no smiles, but very diligent.

As they rode into Bangkok in a taxi, Jeff was amazed again at how modern everything looked. Street lamps lined the eight-lane superhighway. Even though it was almost nine o'clock, traffic was still heavy. Well-lighted buildings and factories stretched along both sides as far as Jeff could see.

"I thought this would all be rice paddies, dirt roads, and mud buildings," K.J. said in awe. "This is cool."

Mindy laughed. "Wait till we get to Vietnam. You'll get your rice paddies, at least outside the cities. And the cities aren't this modern either."

Jeff smiled to himself, knowing Mindy had once again done excellent research for the trip. She would be able to tell them all sorts of facts and stories about the Vietnamese people and their history. Her research always added a lot of insight to the narration scripts she wrote for their videos.

"It's a tragedy the Vietnamese haven't recovered much from the war," Mindy said. "And nobody really won that horrible war."

Jeff looked over at Tom, wondering how he would take her comment. Tom just stared at Mindy, deep in thought.

❖❖❖❖❖❖❖

"Wow," K.J. said, staring up at the enormous seven-story hotel. "Look at this place. I could stay here for a long time."

The hotel was white, and two white elephants stood to either side of the wide front steps.

"That's not a bad idea," Tom muttered. "Maybe we should forget about Vietnam."

Jeff looked at Tom in alarm. Was he going to give up?

"I was just kidding," K.J. said. He threw his camera bag over his shoulder and bent down to pick up his duffel bag off the sidewalk. "I can't wait to get to Vietnam."

"I don't know," Tom worried. "After what just happened, I don't think I'm ready for this."

"We're going to have prayer tonight," Mindy offered. "Somehow, God will get you through."

"And we're with you every step of the way."

Jeff recognized the determination in Warren's voice.

Murals covered the ceiling and high walls of the hotel lobby. A thick royal blue rug stretched out over the huge white marble floor. Jeff could feel the carpet's softness under his feet.

When Warren had checked the team in, a porter escorted them into an elevator lined with exquisitely carved teak paneling.

K.J. beamed. "I can't wait to see my room."

"Our room," Warren shot back, laughing.

"Yeah. You guys can stay here, too."

Mindy groaned. "I just want to see my bed and sleep for hours and hours."

"If we go to bed soon," Warren said, "we should get about eight hours of sleep. Our flight doesn't leave till nine."

The elevator stopped quietly on the fifth floor, and the porter led them down the hall. As the trip coordinator, Jeff had arranged adjoining rooms, with Mindy getting the smaller one. As the porter opened the door, Jeff gasped in delight. It was beautiful. Gorgeous red carpet lined the floors. The beds were huge—maybe king-size. A dark teakwood desk sat along the far wall next to a matching entertainment center. K.J. wasted no time finding the small, fully stocked refrigerator hidden in one of the teak cabinets. All the lamps in the room were brass, and the bathroom floor and walls were cream marble.

"How much did you pay for this place?" Mindy asked.

Jeff grinned. "Not that much. It's nice, but Bangkok has even fancier ones. By the way, K.J., we'll have to pay for whatever you use in that fridge."

"Shoot," K.J. said, putting back a can of soda. "I knew it was too good to be true."

"Let's just take ten minutes to get settled, then meet for prayer," Warren suggested. "K.J., why don't you go down and get us some snacks from the hotel store where they're cheaper. It really has been a long time since dinner."

Mindy grinned. "Prayer, food, and sleep. I can live with that."

"Will you pray with us, Tom?" Warren asked.

Tom nodded. "I need all the help I can get."

❖ ❖ ❖ ❖ ❖ ❖ ❖

A streak of brilliant sunlight shined through the crack in the heavy hotel curtain. It was Friday, the day their adventure would really begin. Jeff rolled over in his bed, not even wanting to open his eyes. Having been on trips like this before, he knew that jet lag was pretty hard to adjust to.

He rolled over again and opened his eyes. K.J. was sound asleep. So was Warren. He propped himself up on his elbow and looked to see if Tom was awake. His spot was empty.

Tom was gone.

Chapter 3

Saigon

Jeff jumped straight out of bed. He tried to stay calm, reasoning that Tom had just gone for a walk. But he had a uneasy feeling it was more than that. He fumbled for a clean pair of shorts. He would have to wake the others, but he decided to do a quick room and hallway search first. After throwing on a white sports T-shirt, he looked out on the balcony, down the hallway, and in the restaurants. Tom was nowhere to be found. Jeff was frantic. He thought at a furious pace. Where had Tom gone? Would they be able to find him in a huge city like Bangkok? And what if they couldn't find him? Was that the end of the trip?

Jeff knew he had to wake the others.

Soon everyone was busy searching. After checking every possible place in the hotel from the lobby to the roof, they met back in the room. No one had found Tom.

Warren gathered everyone together. "Even if we had found him, we couldn't have forced him back. The fight on the plane really shook him. I'm sure you noticed the change in him. I'm sorry to say it, but Tom is probably headed home."

"What are we going to do?" Jeff asked.

"We need to have another prayer meeting. God is the only one who can give the kind of comfort and courage Tom needs to face his past. He's struggling against a whole lifetime of grief and bitterness."

K.J. frowned. "What about our trip and the video project?"

A shadow of worry crossed Warren's face. "It's not what we planned, but God doesn't give up, and neither will we. We still have tickets and visas to Vietnam. We'll just go ahead. Tom's video will have to be scrapped, but we can always work on another film about the needs of Vietnam."

"We can't go without Tom," Mindy cried. "I believe God wants to heal him through this."

"And He still might," Warren agreed. "I'm not sure how strong Tom is spiritually. But if we pray, maybe he'll return."

"We better hurry," Jeff said, looking at his watch. "We have to be at the airport in an hour."

Warren bowed his head and led out in prayer. Huddling together, they each pleaded with God for Tom's return.

❖❖❖❖❖❖❖

Sitting on the Thai Airways air bus, Jeff watched as the seconds ticked by. He knew there was nothing they could do. Tom was a grown man, and he had decided to run.

When his minute hand hit the eleven and there were only five minutes left, Jeff finally resigned himself to the fact that Tom had made his choice. As the last few passengers boarded, Mindy fought back tears. K.J. sat perfectly still, not even having his camera handy. Jeff tried to keep his faith up, but he realized that the plane would be towed out any minute. They would have to go to Plan B. Without Tom.

It was a full flight. He wondered if the empty aisle seat next to him would be given to a stand-by passenger. Maybe it would be given to someone who really needed to be on this flight.

Suddenly, Jeff gasped. Rushing down the aisle with a sheepish grin on his face was Tom. Jeff felt a burst of excitement. Tom sat down beside him. Mindy reached across and grasped Tom's arm. Jeff looked up and whispered a prayer of gratefulness.

"We are so glad you're here," he said, grinning.

Tom smiled. "Thanks."

As soon as the plane reached cruising altitude and passengers were allowed to walk around, Warren and K.J. came over to welcome Tom back. K.J. was excited to have the video project back in the plans.

He bounced on his toes, his dark eyes dancing. "We need to go over the final details of the shoot."

Jeff laughed. "I'm sure you already have it planned perfectly, K.J."

K.J. leaned over Tom's seat. "Are you still up for it?"

Tom nodded.

K.J. took a piece of paper out of his shorts pocket. "If anything makes you uncomfortable, let me know, but here's the plan. First we'll get an interview with you on the plane. After the plane arrives, we'll follow you off. Then we'll meet our host, and Jeff can ask you a few questions. We'll plan different places in Vietnam for more footage. Mindy is already writing the narrative. It's going to be a great shoot. You'll just have to let me know when you want the camera to back off."

Tom nodded. "So far what you said is pretty much the same as before, isn't it?"

K.J. grinned. "Except I'd like to have gotten more footage of our fantastic hotel room in Bangkok."

Even though she knew K.J. was kidding, Mindy reached over to punch him in the shoulder. "You better stay focused, K.J."

❖ ❖ ❖ ❖ ❖ ❖ ❖

Anticipation filled Jeff as the plane started to descend for its approach into Ho Chi Minh City. Now named after the North Vietnamese Communist leader, the city was still recognized by its old name, Saigon. The name was changed in April 1975 when the city fell to the North Vietnamese and the last American helicopters left.

Jeff looked out at the history-filled land below.

The high clouds had cleared, and sunlight filled the sky. His heart was moved thinking of how many Americans had made the flight in but never made it out alive. The good visibility let him see rice fields, bridges across rivers, and wide expanses of rugged terrain. In his mind's eye, he saw the S-shaped country of Vietnam bordered by hundreds of miles of coastland to the east, and surrounded by China, Laos, and Cambodia.

"This country has such a sad history," Mindy said quietly. "The French ruled it for over a century. Then when the Vietnamese people finally got their independence, more trouble started. In 1954, the different sides signed something called the Geneva Agreement, officially dividing the country in two: North Vietnam and South Vietnam. But Ho Chi Minh rose to power in the North. The North was leaning toward the Communist Soviet Union, while the South wanted freedom. In 1975, when Saigon fell and the Americans left, the South was taken over by Communism. North and South became one socialist state."

"And Communism ruled," Tom sighed.

Mindy nodded sadly. "So many people didn't want it. They had given everything to fight it. Remember that famous picture of an overloaded helicopter ready to take off out of Saigon? The door wouldn't shut because one more Vietnamese was trying to squeeze in. He didn't make it. It was an awful day for South Vietnam."

"And for America," Jeff said. He looked down at the green rice fields. He knew Vietnam was one of the poorest countries in the world, and he knew some about the war. But there was so much he didn't know. "Mindy, tell us about this place," he said.

Mindy grinned. She reached into her computer case and pulled out a map. "Over there," she said, pointing to the northern part with a flourish, "is the Red River Delta. It's the heart of the country in culture and history. In spite of all the canals, dikes and embankments, the Vietnamese have never been able to tame the Red River. It creates a lot of flooding."

Mindy pointed to the center of Vietnam. "This is the interior. Once you get away from the coastal belt and the deltas, the land is very mountainous. Vietnam has so much rugged terrain, only a quarter of the land is cultivated. The interior is where the minority hill tribes live. They're called Montagnards."

"I've heard about them," Jeff said. "Some of them have been reached with the Gospel. But there's more work to be done."

Mindy nodded. "Maybe if we ever come to Vietnam again, we can visit some of them." She pointed to the southern part of the country. "Down here where we're landing is the fertile plain of the Mekong Delta. The area provides one of the best places to grow rice. Because of the deltas, the Vietnamese sometimes describe their country as two rice baskets hanging from opposite ends of a farmer's carrying pole. In the north, the Red River Delta forms one basket. The Mekong Delta in the south forms the other. The narrow stretch of land in central Vietnam forms the carrying pole that connects the deltas."

"What exactly is a delta?" Jeff asked.

"A very fertile triangular area of sand and soil

formed at the mouth of a river." Mindy grinned. "If I sound like a dictionary, it's because I looked it up."

"And that's where they grow most of their rice," Tom said.

"Right."

Jeff knew that the Mekong Delta was also where Tom had lost his father. Looking down, he peered into a nation that had once been a deadly war zone. The country had experienced so much military power that the fighting left behind twenty million bomb craters and thousands of ruined lives.

As the jet tires skimmed the ground, Jeff found himself praying for Tom. Tom looked pale but fairly composed for the circumstances. He hoped Mindy's research had helped occupy his mind so he didn't have to sit there worrying.

Mindy leaned over to Jeff. "I hope this jetway doesn't get stuck."

Jeff laughed, glad that the odds of that happening were pretty low.

This time the team exited the plane together so K.J. could videotape Tom's first moments in Vietnam. The first moments were uneventful, but Jeff knew that in this case uneventful was good.

To everyone's relief, getting through customs was fairly simple. Jeff had read that Vietnam welcomed Americans. Of course, it helped that Americans usually had money. But Jeff couldn't wait to experience the genuine friendliness he knew he would find among the people.

Outside in the main waiting area, Jeff looked around for their host. His heart leapt when he spotted a "Reel Kids Adventure Club" sign. By now,

Warren had noticed it, too. Jeff ran ahead to greet the young Vietnamese man holding the sign. He was a very ordinary looking man. Jeff guessed he was about Warren's age. He was dressed casually in jeans and a red shirt, was fairly short, and had dark features, short black hair, and a broad face. What stood out was his smile and how friendly his eyes were—how full of light.

Jeff offered him his hand. "My name is Jeff. I'm a member of the Reel Kids Club."

The others introduced themselves. When it was Tom's turn, he hesitated, not saying anything.

Warren spoke up. "This is Tom Douglas. He's the one who's letting us film his story."

The man smiled at Tom and stuck out his hand. Tom just nodded. Jeff was surprised, but he figured Tom was simply tired and overwhelmed.

"Well," the man said, "I guess you know that I'm Cheng Heng." He smiled. "I know I've talked to Warren on the telephone. I'll be your guide while you're here. It's all arranged for you to stay at our mission house."

"Thank you," Warren said, shaking Cheng's hand again. "We are very thankful to have a friend like you so far from home."

Jeff looked at his watch. It was almost 1:30. "Is it okay if we do a quick interview with Tom before we go?"

Cheng nodded his approval.

Jeff took his cue from K.J. "What made you want to come to Vietnam?"

Tom looked into the camera. "My father was killed in the war. I knew it would be hard, but I also knew I had to come. I hope I made the right choice."

"Where did your dad serve?"

"Around the Mekong Delta. He died along one of the rivers that feeds it."

After a few more questions, Jeff knew it wouldn't be fair to push Tom any further. He wrapped it up. K.J. turned the camera off, and they gathered around Cheng.

"Did I do all right?" Tom asked nervously. "I haven't talked in front of a camera much before."

"You did great," Warren assured him. "You're doing such a generous thing to share your story."

"That's for sure," K.J. said. They all knew Tom was doing a brave thing.

"I want to learn more about all of you and your club, but now I have a surprise for you at my house," Cheng said mysteriously. "We must hurry."

Jeff shot a knowing smile at Mindy. His sister loved surprises.

❖❖❖❖❖❖❖

Cheng's van bounced along the bumpy roads. Warren sat up front, and Jeff sat with Tom on a seat behind Mindy and K.J. The van had room for twelve, so it was only half full. As far as Jeff could tell, Tom seemed to be doing okay. K.J., as usual, was ready with camera in hand.

"We live about thirty minutes from the airport on the outskirts of town," Cheng explained. "Later, I want to take you into Saigon for a tour."

"Great," Warren said. "We're looking forward to it."

Jeff looked around, wanting to take everything in. Scores of bicycles were on the road. "Hey, guys, does this remind you of our China trip?" he asked.

Mindy turned around. "Yeah, it does. I heard there must be at least three bikes for every person in Vietnam. People use them to carry everything."

"How do you always know these things?" K.J. asked.

Mindy grinned. "Research is my thing, just like the camera is yours."

"You're right about that."

"Am I right about the bicycles, Cheng?"

Cheng caught Mindy's eye in the rear view mirror. "Yes, you are. We transport everything on bikes. Pigs, dogs, chickens, steel pipe, cement, truck tires, chairs, and of course rice."

"Wow," K.J. said. "Transportation is a little different in America."

"It keeps us in good shape," Cheng said. "During the war, soldiers even carried weapons and equipment on bikes."

Jeff looked outside, trying to imagine the tanks, trucks, and helicopters used in the war. "Are there any old tanks or weapons still lying around, Cheng?"

"No, not at all. A few years ago you would have seen many, but every piece of metal in the country has been scavenged. That's how many people were injured. Long after the war, they would step on land mines while looking for scrap metal."

K.J. shot Jeff a wide-eyed glance. "Are there any mines still out there?"

"I don't think so," Cheng said. "But you never know."

❖ ❖ ❖ ❖ ❖ ❖ ❖

The mission compound was actually a large red-brick house built during French rule. Cheng was the leader of the mission agency and had arranged the housing for the team. Inlaid mother-of-pearl black-lacquered chests and tables and an old flowered sofa and chair set filled the spacious living room. Beautiful pictures of Vietnamese culture hung on the walls: scenes with boats, water buffalo, people, mountains, and fields.

The bedrooms looked comfortable, too. The first thing Jeff noticed were the mosquito nets draping the beds. He dropped his bags and sank into an old overstuffed chair, pondering all the events that must have taken place over the last twenty years as people adjusted to living under Communism and struggled to rebuild their nation.

Cheng gave everyone a few minutes to get settled, then gathered them together in the living room. "I have a special surprise for you," he said, his eyes dancing. "Please follow me."

Everyone followed Cheng to a closed door. Cheng opened it.

Jeff gasped. A host of bright eyes stared out at them from the darkness.

Chapter 4

Missing in Action

Cheng turned on the light. "Surprise!" he cried in unison with everyone inside.

Jeff looked in shock from Cheng to the smiling Vietnamese faces to a long table filled with food. There was barbecued chicken, beef, fish, and even duck; sweet potatoes, rice, and squash; bananas, apples, melons, tangerines, and fruits Jeff had never seen. He felt himself blushing, realizing all this had been made for them. Mindy looked at him in astonishment. Beautiful smiles radiated from the hearts of all these young men and women who Jeff just knew had to love Jesus.

Grinning, Cheng walked to the head of the table. "These are my friends," he said, sweeping his arm over the room. "They are university students who have committed their lives to Jesus. They help here at our center. They were so excited you were coming that they made this wonderful feast for you."

K.J. had his camera rolling. Two students who knew English brought cool fruit drinks to Warren and Tom and led them to a group of chairs to talk. Jeff felt his heart breaking. It was one thing to hear about the war from an American perspective. It was another to be so close to Vietnamese people who must have been tragically affected. He knew many of them would have stories to tell of parents and relatives lost in war.

K.J. focused the camera on the fruit plates. "What kind of fruit is this?" he asked, pointing to some odd-shaped fruit.

A few of the girls giggled and motioned for Cheng to come translate.

A tall, thin girl named Thi Phuong spoke in Vietnamese. "That is a jackfruit. We have many special fruits in Asia. Mangos, papaya, custard apples, and durians."

Mindy picked up a piece of hairy, red fruit. "What is this called?"

Thi Phuong laughed when Cheng translated. "It is called a rambutan. It's the word for hair. They are very sweet."

"Cool," Mindy said taking a bite.

"We want to make your welcome very special," Thi Phuong said. "After we eat, we will share about our mission and maybe play a few games."

Jeff could hardly look away from the light in Thi Phuong's eyes. Other students came and ushered them through the food line. Jeff talked with those who could speak English and laughed with those who couldn't. Either way, it was great just being together. Pretty soon, Jeff wasn't surprised anymore that the students had worked so hard to welcome them. That's the kind of people there were—generous and full of love and energy.

After everyone had eaten at least one helping, Cheng stood up to get everyone's attention. "This is Mara," he said, when they had quieted down. "She is going to share."

Mara clasped her hands behind her back and smiled shyly. "We are glad you are here. We are so blessed to have a leader like Cheng. Since he started the mission house, many of us have become Christians. We share about Jesus on the university campus and try to help people become established in their Christian life." Cheng translated for the students who didn't understand English.

Jeff felt his heart filling up with the love of God.

Mara went on, losing her shyness as she shared the work she loved. "We also distribute clothes, toys, and food to the poor. We try to help people with whatever they need. We just try to show them Jesus' love. Now will someone tell about your club? We want to hear about *you*."

The others motioned for Jeff to go forward. He shared the purpose of the club, where they had been, and why they were in Vietnam, stopping every few sentences so Mara could translate. When he had answered all the students' questions, Cheng organized a game of charades. They played for an hour, laughing hysterically as they tried to communicate.

Soon it was past five, and many of the students had to leave. While some of the other students cleaned up, Cheng gathered the team together. "Why don't I take you for a quick tour of the city? Then you can all go to bed early."

Jeff yawned.

"That looks like a yes," Warren laughed.

❖❖❖❖❖❖❖

K.J. hung his head out the open window of the long blue van, determined to get footage of the countryside. The wind blew strong against him, but he had a steady hand and a special camera stabilizer. The road was paved but very bumpy.

Jeff couldn't believe how much had happened in the short time they had been in Asia. Tom had been quiet during the party, but so far he was going along with everything.

"Brick is used to build most buildings," Cheng said, pointing toward some homes. "Our soil is of such good consistency it only has to be dug up, shaped into rectangles, and fired in a kiln to make bricks."

"Cool," K.J. responded.

Jeff noticed how the houses crowded right up to the edge of the narrow road. The rice paddies started at the back doors. Like tall blowing grass, they spread out as far as Jeff could see. The paddies were surrounded by water, the lifeblood of growing rice. Water buffalo were in the fields, on the road pulling carts and wagons, in the streams, and even in the front yards.

"I've never seen so many water buffalo in my life," Jeff said.

Mindy laughed. "And look at all those ducks." A farmer was herding ducks across a dry field with nothing more than a long, thin switch.

"We raise a lot of ducks for food," Cheng explained.

Mindy grimaced. "They're so cute."

"Did you know you ate some of those cute ducks today?" K.J. teased. "Cute and tasty."

Cheng laughed. When Saigon came into view, he pointed to the city center. "Downtown Saigon, or Ho Chi Minh City as it is now called, was built by the French. In 1859, it became the capital of the French colony. Later, the French filled in the canals, drained the marshland, built roads, laid out streets and quarters, and planted many trees. The city resembles an old-fashioned French provincial capital. You can see that not everything looks French, though. Many of the rooftops are shaped like pagodas, a popular Asian style, like you see on Buddhist temples."

Warren pointed to a yellow stucco building. "What's that?"

"City Hall. The French built it. Notice all the curves in the architecture. It needs a good paint job, but you can see how fancy it is."

"If that's City Hall, then this must be that street with all the different names I read about," Mindy said.

Cheng was impressed. "You remember well. The French called it Rue Catinat after a French hero no one remembers anymore. Then the Vietnamese dubbed it Tu Do, which means Freedom Street. After Saigon fell to the Communist North in 1975, it was renamed Street of the Revolution. To Saigon residents it's a sad joke because after the revolution, there was no more freedom."

Cheng pointed toward a group of people. "Lots of tourists like to stroll under the trees on Tu Do as it gets cooler."

Jeff couldn't get Cheng's comment about freedom out of his mind. "What's your opinion of the war?" he asked, risking Tom's reaction. He knew they would have to discuss the war a lot more before the trip was over.

"We have many opinions in Vietnam, just like you have in America," Cheng said. "The Vietnamese wanted their independence and finally got it from the French in 1954. But the Communist army in the North came in and took advantage of the South. The Americans came to our rescue but failed to come with full force. It seems the Americans were fighting not to lose, while the North Vietnamese were fighting to win. And they finally prevailed. But when I think of the devastation the war caused, the hundreds of thousands of lives lost, I have to think that nobody *really* won."

Cheng changed the subject. "Ho Chi Minh City still exudes the exciting and bustling atmosphere of the war years. But as you can see, it's in decline. It has been waiting for over twenty years for a prince to come and awaken it with a kiss."

Mindy grinned at K.J., who rolled his eyes.

"Don't look at me," he laughed.

Tom's face was stiff, his eyes angry. He didn't seem to be handling the Saigon tour very well. Jeff tried to think of a way to turn the conversation around, sorry he had asked the question.

"I'm going to find a place to park," Cheng said.

K.J. suddenly got excited. "Look over there." He pointed to the side of the road. "Those bikes are cool."

"Those are called cyclos," Cheng explained. "As you can see, they're bicycle-propelled rickshaws. The drivers hang around hotel entrances, waiting for customers."

Jeff was glad K.J. had lightened things up a bit. They could always count on him for humor or a welcome distraction.

As darkness fell on Saigon, a stream of droning motorbikes and scooters was set in motion. Standing on a street corner, the team saw boys riding with their girlfriends perched sidesaddle on the back seat. On others were entire families. K.J. focused his camera on the scene.

Mindy spotted a woman with a red mouth. "What happened to her?"

"Nothing," Cheng laughed. "She's just eating betel nuts. They're very popular in Southeast Asia, but they stain your mouth red."

Watching a little boy selling a selection of foreign newspapers, Jeff wished he could buy something from him. Another boy held up old coins and trinkets. Sitting next to them was a thin woman holding

a child. Jeff stared in surprise at a brightly painted
cart being pushed in their direction, feeling torn by
all the new sights. The stand had dried octopus on
it, and it rolled to a stop right near them. A tangy sea
smell filled the air. Suspended by strings, the sea
creatures looked like extraterrestrial beings throwing their arms in the air.

"Yuck," Mindy cried. "Gross."

"Hey, I bet they're good," K.J. said. "They'll stick
to your stomach."

Mindy wrinkled her nose. "Well, you can have
all you want, slimy legs and all."

Everyone laughed except Tom. He stood motion-
less, his eyes troubled. Jeff wondered if he was having
an attack in his mind, still imprisoned by memories
of his father's death. Jeff said a silent prayer, knowing God was the only one who could set Tom free.

"I don't know about you," Warren said, "but I'm
getting tired."

Everyone was tired.

On the way back, Jeff slouched down in his seat
and rested his head on the back of the seat. His tired
eyes welcomed the night darkness. Too exhausted to
listen to Warren and Cheng discuss the schedule, he
used the time to pray for Tom. Soon, Mindy's head
bobbed back and forth as she slept sitting up. K.J.
still peered out the window, hoping to find an
unusual sight even in the night.

❖❖❖❖❖❖❖

Lying in bed that night in the room he shared
with Warren, Jeff thought of Tom and K.J. in the next

room. He wanted badly to talk to Tom, but he wrestled to find the right moment. God would have to set it up.

For what seemed like forever, he lay awake thinking about everything he had seen that day. He remembered the things his dad had taught him about wars America had fought in, how soldiers were usually supported and encouraged by people at home. Anger was usually directed at America's enemies. But during the Vietnam War, the American people visibly vented their anger at the American soldiers doing the fighting. Many people opposed the war because they didn't believe America should get involved every time another country went to war. People were also upset because they thought the Vietnam war was being fought half-heartedly.

An image of Tom in an earlier interview haunted Jeff. He could see Tom's anguished eyes, the hurt that hung on. It was a hurt repeated over and over in American and Vietnamese families.

It was no wonder Tom was so confused. Jeff remembered hearing how U.S. politicians even gave speeches against the soldiers' actions. When the soldiers came home, there were no victory parades like after World Wars I and II. Then a U.S. president issued a general amnesty, an Executive Order, pardoning all those who had evaded the draft during the war. Though he had good intentions, it was a final drop of acid in the deep wounds of Vietnam veterans and their loved ones as well as the loved ones of all those killed or still missing. Many saw it as an affirmation of those who had avoided the military. And those who had fought had not even been welcomed home.

Jeff saw Tom's face again. He couldn't think about the war anymore. He fought tears, feeling a little of the pain so many had felt. He knew God was letting him experience His own sorrow over what had happened. Exhausted physically and emotionally, Jeff finally fell asleep.

❖ ❖ ❖ ❖ ❖ ❖ ❖

Jeff awoke suddenly in the middle of the night. His eyes flew open. Someone was shaking him. His head swam for a moment. All he could see was K.J. in a panic.

"What's wrong?" he whispered hoarsely.

K.J.'s eyes were wide in the darkness. "It's Tom."

Jeff sat up with a jerk. "What happened?"

"After you guys went to bed, I was working on my camera. I saw Tom sneaking out of the house. I tried to stop him."

Warren was up and fumbling with the light switch.

K.J. spoke in a rush, still dressed in his clothes from the day before. "Tom said he was hungry and wanted to go out to get a quick bite. He wanted to think things over. He left and asked me not to tell you guys."

Jeff looked at his watch. "It's four a.m. now. Why did you let him go? He was in no frame of mind to go anywhere."

"Hey," K.J. snapped. "I'm not his keeper."

"Did he say where he was going?" Warren asked calmly.

K.J. flopped into the chair by the dark window.

"He just said he'd be back around one. I set my alarm for two and waited. I've hardly slept at all. What do we do now?"

"Saigon is too big to search," Warren said. "We'll just have to wait and hope for the best."

"Should we wake Cheng?" Jeff asked.

Warren shook his head. "Not now."

Thirty minutes passed as the threesome tried to pray.

A distant ring broke the pre-dawn quietness.

K.J. jumped up. "It's the phone."

It rang once more then stopped.

Warren tensed. "Cheng must have picked it up."

They waited in silence, first one minute then two. Heavy footsteps sounded in the hall. Cheng threw the door open, a look of panic on his face. Jeff felt a chill crawl from the nape of his neck to the base of his spine. He knew something was wrong. Really wrong.

"That was the police. Tom got into a fight. They're going to arrest him. They called first to verify his story."

"Where's he at?" Warren asked. "Is he hurt?"

"Not badly. He's at a popular bar in Saigon. The police said they wouldn't arrest him until we get there. But it has to be in thirty minutes. Meet me out front."

Warren pulled a pair of khakis from his suitcase. "There's no time to wake Mindy. She'll have to understand."

Jeff was troubled as he hurriedly switched his sweat shorts for jeans and a T-shirt. "I get the feeling we never should have taken on this assignment."

"I don't know about that," Warren said. "But we will probably have to put Tom on a plane home as soon as possible."

Jeff looked at Warren in surprise. He had never seen him accept defeat so quickly. Jeff had half-expected him to reassure them that everything would work out fine.

"I don't want to give up," K.J. said. "We accepted the assignment because we thought God wanted us to."

"I feel the same way you do," Warren said, "but Tom doesn't seem able to control himself."

Jeff stepped into his tennis shoes and without stopping to tie them followed Warren and K.J. outside. "Do all of Tom's problems mean we were wrong?"

"That's a tough question," Warren said softly. "They might, but sometimes problems don't mean that at all. My only answer is this: God has the power to perform miracles, and He can perform a miracle in Tom."

"That's right," Cheng said, catching Warren's last comment as they climbed into the van.

Cheng already had the van running. Jeff slid the side door shut with a bang. As they sped toward downtown Saigon, his mind flooded with countless thoughts, like the ones he had had at bedtime. He remembered how hard it was for returning veterans to adjust to normal life. They came back different people, changed by the war, and their families and friends often expected them to be the same. The facts ran through his head as they traveled. Some of the vets had ended up in prison. Over seventy percent had ended their marriages in divorce. Some had committed suicide. And all they had done was what they thought was the right thing. Jeff was almost overcome with despair, realizing how terribly difficult it was for anyone touched by the Vietnam War to adjust. He knew only God could do the miracle of healing.

"What kind of bar was it?" K.J. asked. He never could stand silence for long.

"It's been around for a long time," Cheng said, keeping his eyes on the road. "Soldiers used it a lot during the war, so it's quite a popular place. There's always a mix of Vietnamese and American veterans—even a Viet Cong Communist or two."

When they entered the city, the sky was just starting to lighten. Jeff held onto the seat as Cheng raced down Freedom Street. Cheng swung toward the curb and stopped with a jerk. Three police cars lined the curb across the street. Sitting half-dazed on the ground in front of the bar and surrounded by police was a bloodied man.

The bloodied man was Tom.

Chapter 5

Brothers

Jeff couldn't believe it. Tom glanced at the van, then looked away. Knowing it might annoy the police if they made a scene, Warren and Cheng got out calmly. K.J. slid the side door open. Jeff wished he could just stay in the van, but as part of the team he had to get out.

As they crossed the street, Jeff studied the terrible scene. Tom was sprawled on the littered sidewalk, his arms handcuffed behind him. The bar was closed, but a group of men still watched from the street corner. Through the darkened glass of the front window, Jeff saw a janitor mopping up a puddle. The puddle shimmered with pieces of a shattered beer mug. Jeff suddenly felt cold. Someone could have been killed in a fight like this.

Cheng and Warren had approached the police. Jeff and K.J. stood a step back from the others. Listening to Cheng speak Vietnamese made Jeff feel more anxious and helpless. Even when the conversation stretched to ten minutes, Tom stared at the ground, never looking up.

Jeff watched the speakers closely and listened to their voices, wishing he could understand their words. He could tell Cheng was really pleading with the police. Questions ran through his mind. Why did Tom go to a bar? Why this one? Would the police change their minds?

Jeff prayed fervently as Cheng spoke. Finally, a policeman walked over to Tom and loosened the handcuffs. Jeff stared at Tom, wondering if he was dreaming the whole scene. Tom's clothes were ripped. Dried blood was crusted on his face.

The officer helped Tom to his feet. While Cheng shook the officers' hands, Warren led Tom to the van. Jeff and K.J. followed them across the street.

"Do you have any injuries we won't be able to take care of back at the compound?" Warren asked. Jeff recognized the gentle voice Warren used when people were sick or hurting.

Tom shook his head. "Just scrapes and bruises." Without another word, he made his way to the very back seat of the twelve-passenger van and lay down.

Cheng drove back to the compound at a more sane speed. The only sounds as they drove were the whir of the tires on the road and the occasional swish of a passing car. Jeff felt suffocated by the silence. They were halfway home, and the last words spoken were Tom's—"Just cuts and bruises." Jeff had no idea what to say though. Words would not come, and he wondered if they would make a difference anyway.

They were almost to the mission house when Jeff heard Warren ask Cheng what the police had said.

Cheng spoke softly. "They changed their minds. The man Tom fought with was a well-known journalist. He demanded that Tom be arrested. When begging didn't work, I finally put my neck on the line. I promised it wouldn't happen again. If something does happen, the police will hold me responsible."

"Thank you," Warren said quietly. "Thank you."

Jeff looked at K.J. in amazement. Cheng had willingly risked his reputation. Jeff knew then that Cheng had a special love for Tom.

Soon the van pulled into the compound. Tom sat up as Cheng cut the engine. Dried blood matted his dark hair to his forehead. His face was already bruising.

Warren turned around to face the back. "After we get Tom patched up, we're all going back to bed. We need to do some serious talking today." He looked Tom in the eye. "Give me your word you won't leave."

Tom met his gaze and nodded.

As Warren turned around, Jeff met his eye for a split second. Jeff flashed a look of admiration for his leader's ability to stay calm in a crisis and be gentle and firm at the same time. Warren smiled slightly in acknowledgment. Most of the time, Warren let him lead the team, but Jeff was definitely glad that Warren took charge at times like this.

Seeing Mindy run outside to meet them did not make Jeff happy. He knew she would be mad that they didn't wake her up to go with them. He slid the side door open just as she reached it.

"Is Tom all right?" she asked breathlessly.

Jeff looked at her in surprise. She didn't look mad. He suddenly realized what a miracle it was that Tom was okay and that he was *with* them. "Ask him yourself."

Mindy stuck her head in the van and spotted Tom in the very back. "I'm so glad you're here," she said, flashing him a bright smile as if nothing were wrong.

Everyone climbed out of the van. Tom walked ahead with Warren and Cheng to the house.

"What's with you?" K.J. said quietly. "We thought you'd be mad for sure."

"I was," Mindy admitted. "I couldn't believe you guys left without me." She looked at them seriously. "I am part of this team, you know."

"But you're not mad anymore?" Jeff asked.

Mindy shook her head. "I woke up right after you left because some staff people were moving around. They told me what happened. At first I was mad, but I knew God wanted me to pray for Tom. I can hardly believe how much love God gave me for him."

Jeff felt proud of his sister as he watched her run to catch up with the others. "Tom," he heard her say, "I have a first-aid kit, and I promise I know how to use it. Would you let me fix you up?"

Jeff didn't hear Tom's answer, but he followed Mindy into the house like a wounded puppy dog. Jeff was glad his sister was trained in first aid. The only work she loved more than reporting was doctoring.

Cheng brought the mission's medical supplies into the kitchen, insisting that Mindy keep her kit intact for the next emergency. Everyone watched in silence as Mindy sat Tom down on a stool and cleaned his cuts, first to wipe away the dried blood and then to disinfect them. The cuts were minor, except for the one right beneath his hair line. Mindy covered it with a butterfly band-aid.

"Done," she declared.

"And now it's bedtime for everyone," Cheng said, shooing them out of the kitchen.

Jeff went to bed wondering what Tom would get himself into next.

❖❖❖❖❖❖❖

Jeff awoke, confused by the bright sunlight flooding his room. At first he didn't know where he was, but the mosquito netting over his bed quickly reminded him. Then he saw it was after ten o'clock and thought that he had overslept. It wasn't until he saw Warren still asleep in his bed across the room that Jeff remembered everything. The bar. The fight. The police.

He stood up too fast and was instantly dizzy. He had to make sure Tom was still there. Still wearing his jeans and T-shirt from earlier that morning, he raced to the next room. Quietly, he opened the door and stuck his head in. K.J. and Tom were still sound asleep. He closed the door noiselessly behind him and headed back to his own room. The compound was quiet. Only a few staff members currently lived on the premises, and most had left for the day.

Jeff lay on his bed, wrestling with his thoughts and pouring his heart out to God. He longed to see Tom healed, but he felt so helpless. Jeff was beginning to wonder if they would ever make it to the place where Tom's father died. They had planned to go there Monday. Jeff wasn't sure of anything now.

❖❖❖❖❖❖❖

The team was finishing a quiet breakfast of rice, toast, and orange juice when Tom walked into the kitchen.

"I need to share something with all of you," he said quietly.

Jeff was amazed. He sensed something different about Tom. He put his spoon back in his bowl while K.J. wrapped his blanket closer and Warren paused from reading his Bible. Everyone waited for Tom to speak.

Tom looked around the room, first out the window, then at their half-eaten breakfasts, and finally at them. "I'm sorry for the problems I've caused each of you." He took a deep breath, and his voice grew stronger. "I've really struggled inside since I met that guy on the plane. But I realized early this morning that my problem wasn't him. It was me. I've had a raging hatred in my heart for over twenty-one years. With all that hatred, anything could set me off."

Mindy started to get up, then stopped.

Tom smiled at her and went on. "I realize now that I couldn't wait to get to Vietnam to unleash my hatred on the people here." He sat down on an empty chair beside Cheng. "The moment I saw you smiling at the airport, I hated even the sight of you."

Cheng didn't bat an eye.

Tom wiped a tear off his cheek with the back of his hand. "Last night, you were pleading with the police to keep me out of prison. I realized then what a special person you are. I had no right to hate you or anybody else. I see now how much you care."

Unable to hold back anymore, Tom began to weep. Jeff felt hot tears trailing down his own face.

Cheng looked into Tom's eyes. "I helped you because I love you."

Now it was Mindy's turn to choke back tears.

"I heard you in the van last night," Tom said after a while. "I overheard you telling Warren how you put your reputation on the line for me. I don't deserve that kind of love."

Cheng hugged Tom, and Tom began to sob uncontrollably. Jeff couldn't believe it. The miracle he had been waiting for was happening. Tom was letting go of his pain. Cheng held Tom until his sobs subsided.

"I..." Cheng started to say something, then stopped. "I need to share something that none of you are aware of." He hesitated again. "When I heard you were coming, Tom, God put a special love in my heart for you even before you arrived."

Tom stared at him, puzzled.

"You see, Tom, my dad was killed in the war, too."

Mindy took a quick breath, almost gasping. Jeff couldn't control his feelings anymore. He felt God's heart of love filling his own. At that moment, he was filled with pain, love, boldness, and compassion all at once. He wept, not just for Tom and America, but for Cheng and Vietnam. Love seemed to flow around the table. Jeff knew God was healing not only Tom but Cheng, too.

Cheng stood up. "I need to share something else," he said, wiping his eyes. "I'm so sorry for the sixty thousand Americans who died. I'm sorry your dad died, Tom. I'm also sorry for the three hundred thousand Vietnamese people who died from North to South."

Jeff was stunned. Hearing those numbers made him hate war more than ever.

"All of them were either fathers, mothers, sons, or daughters," Cheng said. "All were trapped in the awful grip of war."

Weeping, Tom reached out and hugged Cheng. "I'm so sorry," he said. "I'm so sorry."

Cheng smiled through his tears. "I've learned that there is only one way you can rise above all of this, Tom. You must completely give your life to Jesus Christ. He'll give you His love—a love that gives to those who hurt Him."

Tom sat back down at the table. "I've hurt God for so long. I even thought I was a Christian. But when I saw you standing up for me last night, I realized what a Christian really is—Christlike. And I've learned that whether the war was right or wrong, the real choice I had was to live in bitterness and hate, or love and forgiveness. I've made my choice now because I saw love and forgiveness in action. I want God to give me that kind of heart."

Jeff beamed at Warren. God had used Cheng to answer their prayers. As everyone shared together, Jeff reflected on what a wonderful Saturday it had turned out to be. He knew that they could do the video now and that Tom's perspective would never be the same. Jeff doubted that any of their perspectives would ever be quite the same.

After a late lunch, the team gathered in the living room to plan the next few days. K.J. was so full of energy Jeff almost didn't believe that he had been up most of the night. In fact, K.J. had already been filming some of Tom's fresh testimony.

"Your story is so powerful, " Warren said. "It's a message that needs to get out to thousands."

Tom's response was cut off by the ringing of the telephone. Jeff jumped, remembering the shocking phone call early that morning.

Cheng rushed into the living room. "It's for Tom."

Jeff looked at the others in confusion. Who could be calling for Tom?

Tom went into the kitchen looking more confused than any of them. When he came back, his face was ashen.

Mindy jumped up. "What happened? You look like you've seen a ghost."

Tom sank into a chair. "That was the journalist I got in a fight with—Le Duc Thieu."

"What did he want?" Jeff laid aside the script Mindy had given him to read.

"He's written a newspaper article about our trip. It's filled with lies. He says he'll publish it in the biggest paper unless we pay him three thousand dollars. Today."

Chapter 6

Lies

Jeff felt like he had been hit with a ton of bricks.

"Do you think he's making empty threats?" Warren asked.

Cheng shook his head. "He could pull it off. He's pro-communist and one of the most influential journalists in the country. He knows a lot of people in power."

"What could he say about us?" Mindy asked.

"Lots," K.J. said. "That we're secret revolutionaries. Or spies. Or..."

"Or anything," Tom said in frustration. "It's one thing if I have to suffer because of my stupidity, but now it's hurting you, too. And I can't do a thing about it."

"Maybe you can't," Warren agreed. "But God's bigger than this problem, and He'll help us deal with it. And don't think other people haven't ever suffered the consequences of foolish things I've done."

"Or things I've done," Jeff said.

"Or me," Mindy added.

Tom shook his head, smiling. "You guys aren't going to let me feel bad, are you?"

"Nope," K.J. said.

Tom sat down on the couch. "Well, I need to at least tell you all what happened last night." He took a deep breath and let it out slowly. "I went to that bar because my dad visited there after he arrived in Saigon. He talked about it in letters to my mom. I thought if I went there, I could deal with the pain. I would feel close to my dad."

So that was why he went, Jeff thought.

"After a while, Le Duc came in and we talked. It was a good conversation." Tom hesitated. "I told him why I came to Vietnam. I even told him about your club and the video. He seemed really interested. I didn't know he was a journalist. Then out of the blue he started blaming me and all Americans for the war. I couldn't take it. Finally, I pushed him, and a fight broke out fast. Four or five of his friends started punching me. The police came, and Le Duc said it was all my fault. I still can't believe the police let me go."

Jeff knew from Cheng's expression that they were in trouble.

"What do we do now?" Mindy asked. "The club's reputation will be ruined, and maybe the mission's too."

"He wants three thousand dollars?" Cheng asked.

Tom nodded. "He was very specific. Three thousand U.S. dollars. I tried to apologize, but he just laughed and hung up. He said he'd call back later for an answer."

K.J. shook his head in disbelief. "Where would we get that much money?"

"We won't," Warren said. "We can't give in to bribery or any kind of threats. We'll have to ride this one out."

"Why don't we just call the police and tell them what Le Duc is trying to do?" Jeff asked.

"Because he'll deny the whole thing and turn it against us," Cheng said. "God will have to be the one who vindicates."

"You're right about that," Mindy agreed. "So what's the plan for the rest of the day? If we sit around thinking about Le Duc, we'll go crazy."

K.J. grinned, holding up his camera.

"Well, we know what K.J. wants to do," Warren chuckled. "With Cheng's permission, let's get more history of Vietnam and the war on tape." He smiled at Tom. "We'll give you a break."

"Thanks," Tom said. "I could use one."

❖❖❖❖❖❖❖

Jeff was in the middle of interviewing Cheng when the phone rang. K.J. lowered the camera.

Cheng caught the phone on the second ring. "It's Le Duc," he mouthed, passing it to Tom.

"H-hello," Tom stammered. As he listened, his expression changed from one of fear to one of determination. "I'm sorry," he said firmly. "We won't pay anything. All I can give you is my apology. Hello? Hello?" Tom shrugged and put the phone back in its cradle. "He hung up."

"I'm not surprised," Cheng said. "Rudeness is a good way to intimidate people."

"Well, I feel good about our decision," Tom said. "Actually, I feel better than I did before he called just now."

K.J. looked relieved. "Good. Now we can forget him and work on our plans for tomorrow."

Cheng frowned. "I'm convinced we did the right thing, but I don't think Le Duc will forget so easily. It's like he's on a mission to get us."

"Why don't we give this situation to God?" Warren suggested.

"That's the best idea yet," Mindy laughed. "God can handle Le Duc."

Everyone huddled together.

Jeff led out. "Father, I thank You for the miracle You've done in Tom's life. We know You're at work. Please accomplish Your purpose for the rest of the trip."

Everyone said amen in unison.

"And, Lord," Jeff prayed, "we give Le Duc into Your hands. We know You are more powerful."

Jeff finished, still wondering *how* God would help them and just how far Le Duc would go to get what he wanted.

Warren turned to Cheng. "You have an exciting day planned for us tomorrow. Why don't you fill the others in?"

"I think you'll all like it," Cheng said. "The mission has already scheduled the van, so we'll have to ride the bus tomorrow." He smiled. "I think visitors should always do that in a new country anyway, just for the experience. I've arranged for us to visit a church in the morning. After that, I have a special surprise."

Mindy grinned. "I like your surprises."

❖❖❖❖❖❖❖

It was barely seven o'clock when the team got up to prepare for the busy Sunday. Mindy kept guessing what Cheng's surprise would be.

"Wait and see," Cheng laughed. "Wait and see."

After a quick breakfast, everyone gathered to pray and discuss the day's activities.

"Do you guys see any holes in our video?" Warren asked.

K.J. nodded. "I really think we need to get interviews with U.S. soldiers *and* Vietnamese soldiers. We need both perspectives."

"Good point," Jeff said.

Cheng strode into the living room, his face full of anxiety.

"What now?" Warren asked.

"I just picked up the Sunday morning newspaper."

"Yeah," K.J. said. "Go on."

Cheng held up the paper in despair.

"Oh no," Mindy gasped. "Le Duc cashed in on

his threat. There's a picture of you guys at the bar on the front page."

"He attacked your whole club," Cheng said flatly. "I knew he'd probably follow through, but it still hurts me to see it."

"What does it say?" Jeff pleaded.

"It says that Tom Douglas and a film crew from Los Angeles are visiting Vietnam. He describes you as involved in counterrevolutionary activities, coming with cameras, pen and paper to stir up the people against Communism. He also accuses you of actively presenting the views of American Christianity."

"He's right about the Christianity part," Jeff said.

Cheng went on. "Even your dad's name is in the paper, Tom. He talks about your plans to visit the place he died and your desire to locate his friend Lloyd if he's still alive."

Tom's eyes flashed. "I gave you guys permission to share my story with strangers. I didn't give *him* permission."

"It goes on to talk about how you attacked Le Duc in the bar."

"These are flat out lies," Jeff protested. "How can he say this?"

Cheng shrugged. "He can say whatever he wants. He's a popular journalist with the blessing of the Communist Party."

"Is that the main newspaper?" Warren asked.

"I'm afraid it is."

"That means we're basically history," K.J. said. "Everyone will know about us."

Cheng folded up the newspaper as if he didn't want to look at it anymore. "This will definitely cause some problems," he said. "But most of the Vietnamese people will still be kind to you. They know about propaganda and how it's used to spread lies. But some will not be so kind, especially those who have a grudge against Americans."

"How will we know the difference?" Mindy asked. "And how many are we talking about?"

"Yeah, and what will they do?" Jeff pressed.

Cheng exchanged a worried look with Warren. "We won't be able to answer all of those questions. We'll just have to be wise and accept that this isn't going to be easy."

"Does this change our plans for today?" Warren asked.

"It might change our surprise. I'll have to make a phone call." Before Cheng moved, the phone rang.

"Uh oh," K.J. cried. "I don't like these phone calls."

Cheng picked it up then handed it to Warren. "It's for you."

Jeff watched Warren's expressions. He could tell that it was not good news.

Finally, Warren hung up. "That was the Vietnamese Immigration Authority."

Jeff felt his pulse quicken.

"Even though they don't work on Sunday, they've called a special meeting about us. They want me to come immediately, prepared to give a full explanation of our activities."

Chapter 7

The Buddhist Monks

Jeff couldn't believe it.

Tom began pacing the room, back and forth, back and forth. "This is all my fault. I—"

Warren interrupted him. "We'll all deal with this together, Tom. Le Duc is the kind of person who takes advantage of people when they're weak, like you were that night in the bar. Since then, you've given God your anger and your pain, and last night we gave Le Duc to God, too. Le Duc has no power over us."

Tom stopped pacing. "You're right," he said softly.

Cheng went into the kitchen to make his phone call in privacy. "The surprise is still on, but in a different location," he reported back.

"Good," Warren said. "I guess my plans are changed. You'll have to take charge of the team, Jeff, but ask Cheng for his wisdom as you go. In fact, check with him before you do anything. I'll meet you guys back here tonight."

Jeff nodded.

Warren grinned at Cheng. "Sorry to leave you alone with this bunch."

Everyone jumped when the phone rang.

K.J.'s mouth dropped open. "This is like Grand Central Station."

Jeff felt as though he was holding his breath. Everything was falling apart. When Cheng came back, Jeff had decided he didn't even want to know what the phone call was.

"That was interesting," Cheng said. "It was another very popular journalist named Duan Le. Everyone calls him Donny. He has some pull with the government, but he leans more toward the South's way of thinking."

"So why did he call?" Tom asked.

"He did a story on our mission house once and really liked our work here. He wanted to know if Le Duc's story was true. I briefed him. He said he would keep an eye on it."

"Finally a guardian angel," Mindy cried.

"I don't know about that," Cheng said. "He just wanted to know what was going on."

❖❖❖❖❖❖❖

Jeff was uneasy as they waited for the bus. Even though there were other Americans in Vietnam, he was sure they would be noticed, especially because of the picture.

"Maybe we should disguise ourselves," he said.

Mindy laughed. "Yeah. We would make great looking Vietnamese."

K.J. grinned. "We could shave our heads and get some robes. We could pass as Buddhist monks."

"I'll shave your head," Mindy volunteered.

"No you won't," K.J. said.

Cheng laughed. "Don't worry. There are lots of foreigners traveling here. Many are Americans."

"But they don't look exactly like us," Jeff said.

"No, not exactly," Cheng agreed.

The bus finally pulled up. Jeff was shocked. Except for the normal stares afforded foreigners, most of the people on the bus kept smiling and laughing amongst themselves as the team boarded.

"They must not have read the paper," Tom whispered.

They found seats together at the front of the bus.

Mindy soon found herself giggling. "Why is everyone laughing so much?"

"We love to smile and laugh," Cheng said. "It's contagious, isn't it? My people laugh at everything, including ourselves. Some even laugh if a person's is bleeding. It's a superstition about genies. They feel they can avoid misfortune by throwing the bad spirits into confusion. It's a cultural thing in some places. But laughter keeps us in a good attitude."

"We could use some laughter right now," Mindy said, grinning toward the back.

"Yeah, to confuse the bad spirits," K.J. teased.

Cheng laughed. "We have God to do that for us."

"Can you tell us about the surprise?" Mindy asked.

"Not yet. But let me tell you more about what we're doing first. I'll have to speak quietly."

Everyone leaned closer, straining to hear over the other noise.

"We're going to visit a Vietnamese church today. The government allows for some church meetings. Up until 1993, it looked like things were going to open up. But lately they've been cracking down like they did after the 1975 revolution."

"What happened then?" K.J. asked.

"They wiped out the church and all forms of religion. It slowly came back, but the government required the churches to be licensed. The license meant doing things their way."

The bus hit a deep pothole as it pulled to the side of the road. Jeff nearly slid off his seat. A group of men boarded the stopped bus. They spoke to each other in Vietnamese as they passed by. Then they started pointing at the team.

Jeff felt his face turn red. "What are they saying?"

Cheng looked horrified. "They're telling the rest of the people what the newspaper said about us."

"They must recognize you from the picture," Mindy said.

"I guess it is pretty obvious," Cheng whispered. "Everyone turn and face the front. Maybe the disguise wasn't a bad idea."

Jeff looked straight ahead. The bus buzzed with discussion. Jeff could feel the stares and pointing fingers. Not being able to understand the voices made him feel trapped. After several blocks, the people finally quieted down.

Tom looked sideways at Cheng. "What do you think they'll do to us?"

"I don't know, but we get off at the next stop."

"What if they follow us?"

"Let's hope they don't. It could get nasty."

Mindy's eyes almost exploded out of her brown-rimmed frames. Jeff forced himself to sit still, praying that the bus stop would come soon. Really soon.

After what seemed like forever, the bus stopped. The team filed off and followed Cheng down a dirt road. Jeff glanced over his shoulder. The men had stayed on board.

"We're home free now," K.J. laughed, spinning around to watch the bus disappear into the distance.

"Yeah," Mindy shivered. "For the next five minutes."

K.J.'s camera bag bobbed against his side. "I always wanted to be popular."

"Well, you got your wish," Mindy said.

The team strolled toward a little church almost hidden in the trees. The white paint was peeling off its small steeple.

"This must be really old," Tom said.

Cheng nodded proudly. "We're lucky to have some of these old churches. There's a lot more freedom in South Vietnam than in the North. We don't know how long that will last."

"Are the Christians committed?" Mindy asked.

"Some say the organized church is weak. But if

you even declare yourself to be a Christian, you are taking a real stand in a Communist country."

They stopped in front of the church. A few people had just gone in the open door. A slender Vietnamese man wearing a white shirt, a plain black tie, and black pants hurried outside as if he had been waiting for them.

"He's not smiling much for a welcoming party," K.J. muttered to Jeff.

Jeff elbowed him. "Shh."

"This is the pastor," Cheng said, taking a few steps to greet the anxious looking man.

After a short exchange with Cheng, the man smiled apologetically at the team and went back inside.

Cheng looked disappointed. "I'm so sorry. Because of the newspaper story, he's asked us to leave. He feels it wouldn't be wise for us to attend now. He expressed his deepest apology. I know he was really looking forward to our visit."

Jeff trailed behind the others, back down the dirt road. "Now I know what it feels like to be a fugitive."

K.J. laughed. "Kinda like that movie where a one-armed man's on the run, trying to hide."

As soon as K.J. said it, Jeff realized it wasn't funny. In Vietnam, it wasn't unusual to see someone who had lost an arm or leg.

"I'm sorry, Cheng," K.J. said, realizing that a one-armed man would have no trouble hiding in Vietnam.

"It's okay," Cheng said smiling.

K.J. smiled back in relief.

Cheng stopped where the dirt road met pavement. "Let's head back to the bus."

"Oh no," K.J. groaned. "Not that."

Cheng reconsidered. "You're right. Maybe that's not a good plan. Let's try to catch a taxi. The main road isn't too far in the other direction. My surprise isn't scheduled until three."

"What do we do till then?" Mindy asked.

Cheng put his hands out and shrugged. "God must have something planned."

People sped by on heavily loaded bicycles. The team walked slowly down the road, not in any hurry. Rice paddies soaked in standing water spread out like tall, rich grass on both sides of the road. To Jeff they looked like beautiful green blankets. Tiny brick homes dotted the lush landscape.

Suddenly, Jeff heard voices nearby.

"Welcome to Vietnam."

Jeff turned around. Across the road, under a big shade tree, sat two men with shaved heads. They wore sandals and golden brown robes that exposed one shoulder. Both had books open on their laps. One man wore glasses and looked younger than the other.

Cheng went over to greet them. They all followed. After talking with the men a while, Cheng turned back to them.

"These men are Buddhist monks. They're very interested in practicing English. They asked to talk to you."

Jeff was excited. He wondered if this was the divine appointment Cheng had mentioned earlier. "Will they understand us?" he asked.

"Yes," Cheng said, smiling at the men. "But they want to practice listening and speaking."

"Do they know who we are?" Mindy asked softly.

"They said they recognize us, but I told them the article was full of lies. Let's talk to them."

K.J. was already moving to sit next to the men. The others gathered around under the tree, glad to sit in the shade after their long walk. Jeff tried to recall the things he had learned about Buddhist teachings. He remembered that Buddha was born in Nepal in 563 B.C. to a rich family, and that he grew up with a passion to help people who were sick and in pain. It was on Buddha's fourth travel that an old man persuaded him to become one who seeks answers to why man exists on Earth. Jeff recalled how Buddha thought he had discovered why people suffered. Believing there was a wheel of life, or karma, he concluded that the sum of a person's actions in one life must be paid for in his next life. A constant cycle of life would occur, allowing one to improve himself in each life by doing good deeds.

Jeff's excitement grew as Cheng introduced the club.

"We are glad to meet you," the young man said. "You have become well known quickly."

Jeff smiled. "But not in a good way. We're sad because we wanted to make new friendships with the Vietnamese people."

The older monk closed his book and laid it on the grass beside him. "We are followers of Buddha."

"We're followers of Christ," Mindy said simply.

"I'm curious," K.J. said. "What do you have to do to become a monk?"

The young monk looked pleased that K.J. had asked. "It requires three things," he explained. "First, we must give up all earthly possessions and beg for our daily living. Second, we must never inflict suffering on someone else. And third, we must not marry."

K.J. grinned. "That sounds pretty hard—especially the single part. And it seems like I'm always hurting people's feelings when I don't mean to."

"We live this way because we believe in the teachings of Buddha," the older monk said. "It's not all hard. Our needs are supplied and the people respect us."

Jeff took a chance. "Would you mind if we talked with you for a while about our beliefs?" he asked.

"Speak," the older man said. "We will listen."

Mindy caught Jeff's eye. Jeff nodded at her, realizing that she wanted to share. He knew she had done her homework on Buddhism, the strongest religion in Vietnam and Southeast Asia.

"My sister will share," he said. He leaned back on his arms to listen, beginning to wonder if these men wanted to learn more than English. The grass tickled his wrists.

Mindy's eyes were full of life. After sharing her testimony, she talked about the one true God who promises eternal life. Jeff knew she wanted to show them that there wasn't a cycle of life, but one lifetime and one God. She shared how all the good deeds in a thousand lifetimes wouldn't do any good without Jesus.

Hoping that the men would really think about what she was saying, Mindy finished. "Man's suffering is because of the fall of God's perfect creation and ongoing sin in the world. The problem of suffering will never be solved completely until Jesus returns."

The young monk smiled. "She is very good," he said. "Tell us more."

Jeff was amazed at their openness. He began telling them of Jesus' love, and soon all the team members, including Cheng and Tom, were sharing. The monks listened intently.

"We must leave soon," Cheng said when there was a pause in the conversation. "It's almost 1:30."

The monks looked as surprised as Jeff felt. They had been talking for over two hours.

"Do you mind if we pray for you before we leave?" Mindy asked.

"Please," the older monk replied.

The young one nodded. "We would be grateful."

They all bowed their heads. Mindy expressed her heart, asking God to bless the men and reveal Jesus to them as the true Savior.

Jeff felt proud of his sister as they continued their walk up the road.

"We need to flag down a taxi," Cheng said. "Let's wait over there."

Just then, a car swerved toward them. A group of angry men stared out the windows, pointing.

Chapter 8

The Mysterious Message

The car skidded to a stop a foot from Jeff, its spinning tires throwing gravel up from the edge of the road.

The dust stung Jeff's eyes. "What do we do?" he shouted.

"All of you stand back," Cheng commanded. "I'll see what they want."

The passenger in the front seat rolled down his window. He and the driver started shouting at Cheng at the same time. Jeff could hear the anger in their voices.

The men were still talking when Cheng turned

back to the others. "They recognize us. They said they won't bother us if we give them money."

"Is that what it's about?" Jeff asked. "How much do they want?"

"Give them twenty dollars."

Jeff struggled to decide what to do.

"Bribery is a way of life for some people," Cheng said. "You'll find it in all countries—greed is the same everywhere."

Jeff nodded. He pulled out a twenty dollar bill and handed it to Cheng. He hated the thought of giving the bribers a penny, but he knew their lives might be in danger.

Before Cheng could step back toward the car, a taxi came around the corner. Cheng raised his hand and waved it wildly. "Keep your eyes on the car and run back this way. If the taxi stops, get in quick."

Jeff imagined the men getting out of their car or throwing it in reverse or...

The taxi pulled over twenty feet behind the bribers. Seeing that it was empty, Jeff yanked open the back door, Cheng the front, and the team piled inside. Cheng gave the driver directions.

"That was close," K.J. cried from the front seat. "What are we going to do for the next week and a half?"

Mindy's eyes flashed in indignation at the bribers. "We can't let them intimidate us. Let's get on with the job God has called us to do."

Jeff leaned his head back on the seat, breathing hard. "You're right. It would be easy to stay at the mission house and hide. But that's exactly what the enemy wants us to do. Tomorrow we'll do some more shooting and head to the Mekong Delta to visit..." Jeff stopped. He didn't want to upset Tom.

Tom smiled. "I'm okay now, really. It will be hard, but I'm looking forward to going there. I want to put these painful memories to rest."

"I believe you will," Jeff said. "I know you will."

"Are we going to get our surprise now?" Mindy asked.

Cheng laughed. Mindy grinned back, and everybody started laughing. Jeff was just glad to be in the safety of a taxi cab.

Cheng directed the driver to turn. After a bumpy ride down a dusty road, he ordered the taxi to stop.

"We're getting out here," he said over his shoulder.

"This is the middle of nowhere," Mindy teased. "I was hoping for an ice cream parlor."

"With no people there," K.J. added.

Everyone laughed.

Jeff watched Cheng pay the taxi driver with American dollars. He remembered that it was easier to pay for things with dollars than with credit cards or Vietnamese dong. Like other countries, Vietnam liked American currency.

Cheng became very serious. "We need to be careful no one is watching. We're going to walk about a quarter of a mile."

Jeff exchanged curious glances with Mindy. "Where are we going?" he asked. "And why so secretive?"

"You'll see," Cheng said. "Just trust me."

They walked without talking, seeing nothing but rice paddies and a few birds. At last they came upon an old farmhouse. After looking both ways, Cheng motioned for them to follow him around to the back door. Cheng knocked. Jeff shifted his weight from one foot to the other. He couldn't wait to solve the mystery. Finally, the door opened. A short, stocky man dressed in slacks and a white shirt stood behind it. When he saw Cheng, he smiled. After the men exchanged a few words, the team hurried inside. Jeff looked at Mindy in shock. They knew now what the surprise was. Cheng had taken them to a special underground church meeting.

Cheng smiled at the team, knowing they were pleased with the surprise. "These are my friends from America," he announced. "This is Mindy, Jeff, Tom, and K.J."

Jeff shook hands with a dozen smiling believers.

"I'm not allowed to tell you their names," Cheng explained. "Just greet them with brother and sister."

As Jeff looked into the eyes of the men and women, he knew why they risked everything to attend meetings like this and share God's love with others. They were in love with Jesus.

The leader said something, and everyone sat down. Cheng translated as the leader continued to speak. "He's very glad you're here and very saddened by the lies spread about us. They've been praying for you and our mission. After worship, he wants the team to share."

Cheng translated for Jeff. "We'd be glad to. This is one of the best surprises we could have. We've heard about your love for Jesus, and now we can see it in your faces."

They spent an hour worshiping God in the shabby white farmhouse. Tears flowed freely from their faces as the people sang with their whole hearts. Afterward, the leader invited the team to share. Each member went forward and spoke for a few minutes with Cheng translating. As Jeff spoke, he wished he could know each person's story. He knew that if it weren't so dangerous the members could teach the team so much.

Before Jeff sat down, he introduced Tom. "I want you to meet the person responsible for us coming here. His name is Tom. He's the one talked about in the newspaper article."

Jeff noticed Tom's nervousness as he stepped forward. He wasn't used to speaking before groups, but as he shared the story of how God recently touched his life, everyone was captivated. Tom talked of love, acceptance, and forgiveness. He spoke of believers being brothers and sisters and finally of how God's love could transcend hatred, even hatred caused by war. By now he had lost all of his nervousness.

As Jeff felt the love flowing between Tom and the Vietnamese people, he felt he'd had a glimpse of what heaven would be like.

After more worship, the leader invited the team to eat with them. A special meal of baked fish, rice and sweet potatoes was laid out in the kitchen. When Jeff saw the food, he realized that they hadn't eaten anything since leaving the mission house that morning. The pastor insisted that they go through the line first and kept telling them to take more.

Cheng grinned as he translated. "More, more. Take another spoonful."

They went back into the other room to eat. Someone had pulled all the chairs into a circle.

Jeff balanced his plate on his lap. "Can you tell us a little about the underground church?" he asked after taking a few bites.

Cheng translated.

The pastor wiped his mouth with a napkin. "We have to be very careful. I am happy to tell you what I can. God is working here. House churches are being planted in many places. There are churches among the fifty-four tribal groups, and they are all growing. We all experience great opposition, but it only makes the movement stronger."

The team listened with excitement.

"The government is cracking down on us," the pastor said, "but it only drives us to our knees. We need your prayers, but you must be careful not to share much detail with others."

Mindy smiled. "We feel very privileged to be with you. We'll pray for you and ask others to pray for you, too. But we'll be careful not to hurt you."

❖❖❖❖❖❖❖

The team walked toward a taxi stand that Cheng said was just ahead.

"I'm so glad you took us there," Tom said. "I can't believe these are the same people I've been hating all my life."

"Wasn't it awesome to hear them sing in Vietnamese?" K.J. asked. "I kept wishing I could record it."

"I hope it wasn't too dangerous for them," Jeff worried, thinking of how one of the men had taken the extra risk to drop them off near the main road.

Cheng walked quickly, knowing everyone was anxious to meet Warren back at the mission house. "I hope not, too," he said. "After the newspaper article appeared, I called the leader to cancel. But he wouldn't take no for an answer. He changed the location instead."

"Do they usually let visitors come?" Mindy wondered.

"No, actually they don't. You are right to be concerned. It's not wise to visit underground house groups. A number of foreigners have gotten our people in trouble. We went only because they invited us."

"I take it we shouldn't say anything about them in the video," K.J. said.

Cheng shook his head. "You must not write or put anything on the video about the meeting. This was my surprise just for you."

"Those people are totally committed," Mindy said in awe. "They're the hope and future of Vietnam."

❖❖❖❖❖❖❖

It was past seven and Warren still hadn't come back to the mission house. Mara and Thi Phuong had been waiting for the team when they got back from the underground church. They were concerned about the newspaper article. Now they were gone and everyone was just relaxing around the living room. Jeff tried to read, but he kept wondering what was happening at the immigration office.

Finally, an hour later, a taxi stopped in front of the mission. An exhausted looking Warren stepped out.

Jeff went out to meet him. "Boy, you look like you've had a rough day."

Warren nodded. He looked completely worn out, even sick. "Come inside. I'll tell everybody all about it."

"I've never been through such a grilling," Warren said, sitting down in the living room." They asked me every question in the book. Their plan was to pull our visas and throw us out of the country tonight."

"What happened?" Tom asked, wide-eyed. "Did that change?"

"After hours of probing questions, they finally believed me. They even apologized for the inconvenience."

Mindy's computer lay forgotten on her lap. "Is someone going to write another article and change the story Le Duc wrote about us?"

Warren leaned back in the flowered recliner. "No. They can't do anything about that. But they assured me that we shouldn't have any trouble outside the city. The newspaper is distributed only in the main cities."

"That's good news," Cheng said. "Now all we have to do is convince the other half of Vietnam."

Everyone smiled.

"It might be a good idea to lay low tomorrow," Warren said. "We'll work on the video. Then Tuesday morning we'll get an early start for the Mekong Delta."

"We'll be going by van and then by boat," Cheng said. "It's all arranged."

Jeff looked uneasily at Warren. He was too pale.

❖❖❖❖❖❖❖

Monday afternoon, the team busied themselves preparing for the video shoot the next day. Mindy worked on adding material to the interviews by briefing Jeff on information she had researched. It added so much depth to their work. K.J. shot some footage of the compound and worked on ideas for editing the video once they got home. Jeff fine-tuned the narration script. Cheng was busy catching up on his business. Last Jeff knew, Tom and Warren had gone for a walk. Warren had been feeling tired and decided that some exercise might help.

From the living room, Jeff noticed an old green car stop in front of the compound. A heavyset man got out and came toward the front door. Cheng answered his knock.

"I'm looking for Tom Douglas," the man said, speaking excellent English.

"I'm sorry. He's not here." Cheng looked worried. "May I ask who you are and what you want?"

The man smiled, showing darkened front teeth. "My name is Ho Lang. I read the article about Mr. Douglas and the club he's traveling with. I am sorry for the reporter's rudeness. I'm here to help, Mr. Douglas. May I wait?"

Cheng hesitated.

"They're coming now," K.J. said, nodding toward the window.

Tom and Warren were coming up the path. They stepped inside, looking puzzled.

"Someone's here to see Tom," Cheng said.

The man stuck out his hand. "I'm Ho Lang."

"Tom Douglas."

"May we sit down?" Mr. Lang asked.

"Sure," Cheng said. "Please do."

Jeff cleared the scripts off the couch.

"I understand from an article in the newspaper that your father had a friend named Lloyd Thompson who fought in the war with him," Mr. Lang said.

Tom nodded.

"And he's been missing since 1973?"

"Yes," Tom said.

Mr. Lang looked Tom in the eye. "I have reason to believe he's still alive."

Chapter 9

The River Ride

Jeff couldn't believe his ears. He had heard reports of MIAs and POWs ever since he could remember, so he understood what the famous initials meant: Missing in Action and Prisoner of War. His dad had even anchored news stories about people who thought that some American soldiers were still alive in Vietnam—soldiers whose families thought they were dead. But now he was hearing a real-life story.

Tom looked stunned. Speechless, he stared at Mr. Lang.

Cheng broke the silence. "What proof do you have to make us believe you?"

"Good question," Mr. Lang said. "After the newspaper article appeared, a friend in Hanoi called me. He told me he knows where Mr. Thompson is— in some kind of prison camp in the North. He also said he has proof."

Jeff looked at the others and saw his own disbelief mirrored on their faces. Tom sat on the edge of the couch, still in a state of shock. Finally, he responded.

"Lloyd was the closest friend my dad ever had. He was with my dad when he died. He kept writing my mom until April of '73. After the letters stopped coming, my mom found out that the government had listed him as a POW. Finally, he was put on the Missing in Action list."

"Is it possible that he could still be alive?" Warren asked.

Tom shrugged. "The U.S. government reports 2,260 Americans still missing. After all the films on Vietnam came out, people put lots of pressure on the government to keep searching. In Hanoi, there's a military office called the U.S. Task Force-Full Accounting Office. Their job is to find MIAs, dead or alive. Many people believe that some men are being held in remote places or that they're hiding out and living with the Vietnamese."

Mr. Lang shifted impatiently in his chair.

"So how can I find him?" Tom asked. "Who can help us?"

Mr. Lang pulled a piece of paper out of his shirt pocket. "This is the address of my contact in Hanoi. He has specific information."

Tom looked at Warren and Cheng. "I owe it to my

dad to give it a try—whatever it takes. I've been in touch with Lloyd's family in Arizona recently, too."

K.J. looked bewildered. "We weren't planning to go north. Does this change everything?"

"I could go there alone," Tom offered.

Warren put his hands up to signal no. "We'll talk about this later. Right now let's get the information we need."

Jeff frowned. Warren looked pale, as if the walk hadn't done him any good.

Mr. Lang cleared his throat. "The fee is very small."

"I knew it," K.J. muttered. "This guy is after money like everyone else."

Tom looked annoyed. "Of course there's a fee. How much will it cost?"

Mr. Lang studied the scrap of paper. "To give you this, only fifty dollars. After you see the proof in Hanoi, my contact will require a fee if you want to pursue the search."

Without hesitation, Tom pulled his wallet out of his back pocket. Jeff wanted to stop him, but it was too late. Tom counted the money out to Mr. Lang and took the slip of paper with the address.

"We've got us an adventure now," K.J. said after Cheng showed Mr. Lang to the door. "I guess we're going to Hanoi."

Warren grimaced, holding his stomach.

"Are you okay?" Jeff asked. "You don't look so hot."

"I don't feel so hot," Warren admitted. "We haven't made any decisions about this yet, K.J. We'll pray about whether we should go to Hanoi."

"What about the newspaper article?" Mindy asked. "People might know about us in Hanoi."

"We'll cross that bridge when we get there," Jeff said.

K.J. laughed. "I've heard there are some cool bridges there."

Jeff rolled his eyes at his friend.

"What do you think, Cheng?" Warren asked.

"It's a long shot. There have been sightings of Americans, but very few. Among the Vietnamese, North and South, three hundred thousand are still missing. War has a way of making people disappear."

"That guy is after the bucks," K.J. insisted.

Tom looked irritated. "Look. It's only money. My uncle is very well off, and he gave me more than enough for the video and other expenses. I'll cover the two-hour plane ride to Hanoi and any other fees. I've got to give it a chance."

"Why don't we pray about it now?" Warren suggested. "If God says okay, we can go on Thursday after our return from the Mekong Delta and the video shoot at the tunnels."

"Okay," Jeff said, "let's pray and see if God gives us a peace about it."

Warren groaned, bending forward. "I'm sorry. I must have eaten something really bad, or maybe I'm coming down with the flu. I need to lie down."

Tom and Jeff got off the couch.

"Here," Tom offered, "lie down here."

Jeff leaned a throw pillow against the arm of the sofa. "Are you going to be all right? We need you on this trip. It's getting a little scary."

"I'll be fine," Warren assured him, lying down. "I

just need a good night's sleep. I'll go to bed as soon as we pray."

"Are we going to pray silently?" Mindy asked.

Warren nodded. After a few minutes, Jeff had his answer: yes. He waited quietly.

"What do you all feel you got from the Lord?" Warren asked.

K.J. nodded yes. Jeff nodded. Mindy nodded, too.

"What about you, Cheng?"

"As I was praying, I got a picture in my head of a big bamboo cage and an American inside."

Mindy's eyes widened. Jeff raised one eyebrow.

"I received a strong leading to go north," Mindy added. "I believe whether this is a true or false report, we need to go to Hanoi."

"Boy," Warren said. "That was easy. I have a peace that we're to go. We'll have to be careful, but God must be up to something."

"You know," K.J. said, "this isn't why I said yes, but getting footage of the North's headquarter city will really help the video."

Jeff laughed to himself. K.J. was *always* thinking of the video.

"If we've all agreed," Cheng said, "I'll call the travel agency and see if there are flights available for Thursday."

Streams of golden light filled Jeff's room. He opened his eyes, trying to remember why he felt so excited. *The Mekong Delta.* Today was the day they would ride the boat upriver to the Mekong Delta. Today was the purpose for their whole trip.

Jeff switched off his alarm and got out of bed. For some reason, maybe excitement, he had woken up before it even went off.

Relieved to see that Warren was already up, Jeff headed to the bathroom off their room. He was not prepared to see Warren sitting on the floor by the toilet.

He stopped in the doorway, horrified. "Are you okay?"

Warren looked up, his eyes bloodshot. "I've been throwing up all night. It must be what some people call the Bangkok Trot. There's no way I'm going to be able to go with you guys today."

"You must be miserable."

Warren gripped the counter and pulled himself up. "Very. You'll have to work with Cheng to lead the team. I'll have to sleep this off." He leaned over the sink and splashed cold water on his sweaty face.

Jeff fought back fear. He knew that Warren had trusted him before and that God had always come through. He would have to depend on God.

Warren stumbled back to bed. "Cheng will be very helpful. The most important thing is to watch Tom closely. He is not going to have an easy trip."

"I'll watch him," Jeff promised. "Now get some sleep so you can go with us to Hanoi."

Jeff dressed quickly. He would have to tell the others Warren couldn't go.

❖❖❖❖❖❖❖

The morning was already hot as they drove toward the Mekong Delta. K.J. went around opening all the van's windows.

Mindy leaned over to Jeff. "Isn't it great how they're becoming friends?" she said softly.

"It's awesome," Jeff agreed, looking up front at Cheng and Tom.

The two hadn't stopped talking since they started the hour-long trip to the city of My Tho at the edge of the delta. In My Tho, they would rent a boat and go up the river to the place north of Vinh Long where Tom's dad had died.

"Hey, Cheng, did you get the tickets to Hanoi?" K.J. asked.

Cheng kept his eyes on the road. "Finally. I had to call again and again. Sometimes things get a little complicated here. At first my travel agent couldn't get them, but then he said he could get them for twenty dollars extra."

"How can they get away with that?" Mindy asked.

"It's not right, but we view it as paying a little more. If my nation would find God, we could set up rules of right and wrong. Perhaps even our driving habits would change."

"This is intense," Jeff agreed, staring at all the bicycles, tractors, trucks, and speeding cars. "But I've seen some pretty wild drivers in California."

Mindy laughed. "Wait till K.J. gets on the road."

"Hey, I'll be a good driver. I don't want to end up in an accident on the highway."

"Tell us what you know about the Mekong Delta, Mindy," Cheng said.

Mindy grinned. "You know more than I do, but sure. Where the delta is, the Mekong River drains into five branches that flow into the sea. The delta is one of the great rice bowls of Asia, and it produces half of Vietnam's rice."

"I've heard of bread baskets," K.J. laughed. "But a rice bowl?"

Cheng swerved the van onto a dirt lot at the edge of the road. Jeff looked at K.J. and Mindy in confusion. A teen-age girl sat beneath a thatched lean-to, hunched over the polished black and silver of her foot-powered, treadle sewing machine. Jeff remembered seeing a picture of his great-grandmother using something like that. For a moment, he thought he was in a time machine.

The young woman was intently focused on keeping the hem straight on the garment she was sewing. On a handcrafted table beside her was a line-up of beverages, mostly locally bottled fruit punch. Jeff recognized some Coke cans, too. On the shelf below the canned and bottled drinks was a selection of local delicacies: fresh fruit, a dried fish, rice balls, and several things Jeff didn't recognize. Between the girl's seat in the shade and the sun-soaked road was a five-gallon can with a one-liter plastic bottle next to it.

Cheng looked back to see their reactions. "It's a gas station," he laughed, opening his door. "I decided I better get a couple of liters here to hold us until we get on a main highway. Go ahead and get out. Let's get a beverage, too."

❖❖❖❖❖❖❖

The boat docks in My Tho were already bustling with activity. Boats were being washed, engines tinkered with, and fishing nets tied, as people prepared for work on the river.

K.J.'s camera bag bounced with every step. "I love getting on boats. It has a sense of adventure to it."

"And no one knows us out here," Mindy said. "They'll probably think we're European or Russian tourists. Just don't talk too loud, or we'll give it away that we're Americans."

Cheng pointed up ahead. "The boat rental place is right there."

Jeff stared in surprise at the dock Cheng was pointing to. Scores of boats stood on racks, end on end. A few more were already in the water. They were old looking boats, needing paint and probably repair. When the proprietor showed them the boat they would use, Jeff wondered if it would make it up the river. The sixteen-foot faded brown boat was tied to the dock. It had torn cushion seats, chipped paint, and a rusty looking engine.

As they prepared to board, Jeff noticed two Vietnamese men arguing back toward shore. One man seemed to be staring at the team. The other man grabbed his arm, but he jerked away and started to walk down the dock.

A heavy fear gripped Jeff. He looked down at their boat, still being prepared. The pilot was having trouble starting the engine. Cheng was down in the boat talking to the pilot, and the others were all sitting on the edge of the dock, watching. Jeff prayed as the man strode toward him, trying to telling himself he was silly for over-reacting.

Finally, the pilot got their boat started. Seemingly at the same time the man turned away. He walked back up the dock and got in a small boat with his companion.

Jeff told himself that Le Duc's article had made him paranoid.

"Come on and get in," Cheng called. "Do you guys have everything?"

K.J. held up his camera bag. "I have everything I need."

"Let's go then," Cheng said.

❖❖❖❖❖❖❖

After thirty minutes, Jeff was beginning to trust that their boat would make it. He had decided that he would for sure tell Cheng if he saw the men again. They were moving down one of the branches of the Mekong River, something Jeff could hardly believe. He could hardly believe he was in Vietnam at all.

Dotted with lopsided palm trees, the shore rose steeply from the water here. The jungle loomed large in the background. Muddy banks made the water murky and dark. Large fishing boats moved alongside smaller boats carrying whole families. In some, women in pointed straw hats rowed along-side happy children. The only noise was the roar of boats and wind.

Jeff had checked behind them for the two strange men, and he hadn't seen them. Sitting next to K.J. on a cushioned bench in the bow, he tried to imagine what it must have been like during the war. Before the trip, his dad had briefed him on the newscasts that had been shown nightly in America. Many newscasts were from the Mekong Delta area. Jeff imagined helicopters skimming over the trees and soldiers traveling on big boats up and down the waterways.

He thought about the million Vietnamese who fled the country on boats after the war. They were known to the world as "boat people" because of their dangerous and deadly escape from South Vietnam across the seas. Drownings in the ocean were a regular news item.

With his face to the warm wind, he thought of the many soldiers who must have traveled the same river. They had learned to expect death around each bend of the river, and if not there, then from above. The thought made Jeff uneasy.

Feeling on edge, he checked behind them for the men he had seen on the dock. *One last look*, he told himself.

Wait! There they are! Jeff was terrified. The small boat the men were in had been hidden behind a larger fishing boat.

Chapter 10

The War Zone

Jeff nudged K.J. and turned carefully around on the bench to face the stern. Cheng was sitting with his back to them, facing Mindy and Tom.

"I think we've got company," Jeff whispered, pointing at the boat. Mindy and Tom leaned forward to listen. "I didn't want to say anything, but they were watching us on the dock. One of them started to walk over to us. He jumped in his boat when our boat started."

Cheng frowned. "One of the guys is taking a picture. I wouldn't be surprised if they work with Le Duc."

"Well, as long as they're just taking pictures, it's okay with me," K.J. said.

"We need to watch them carefully," Cheng told them. "Whether they're news people or from the government, we'll just have to stay calm."

Mindy looked worried. "For your sake, Tom, I hope they take their pictures and get lost. You deserve not to be bothered after all you've been through to get here."

Jeff watched the men's boat in frustration. He didn't want anything to distract Tom from having a special time alone when they got there. He tried to relax. As they traveled, the brush along the shore grew thicker and the jungle darker. The sun was high in the sky over the river.

"Mosquitoes!" K.J. cried. "Get the can of repellent."

Jeff heard a familiar buzzing noise.

Cheng reached into his bag and handed K.J. the can.

K.J. sprayed his exposed skin and passed the can on.

"This is why we had to get all those awful shots," Jeff said, swatting at the insects.

"And did they hurt," Mindy groaned.

The boat slowed a bit. Even after all the commotion over the mosquitoes, Tom was really quiet.

"You okay?" Jeff asked.

"I'll be okay," Tom said. "I'm realizing this is the place my dad…" His eyes began to fill with tears.

Jeff looked helplessly at Mindy.

"It's okay," Tom said, seeing their concern. "My father was a Christian, and I'm just beginning to really understand what that means. Somewhere right here, he departed for heaven."

Hearing these words thrilled Jeff. He knew God was doing a deep work. For so long, Tom had kept his emotions inside. Jeff had learned from his parents how important it was to grieve and let emotions out. After everything he had seen and experienced on this trip, Jeff felt full of emotion, too. He couldn't imagine all the frightening days and terrifying nights the soldiers had faced. Jeff had seen war movies, but he couldn't imagine soldiers cutting through this jungle carrying eighty pounds strapped to their backs. Helmets, flak jackets, weapons, grenades, food and water, first aid—Jeff couldn't comprehend it. He wiped the sweat from his forehead. As the boat slowed, the heat grew and the air hung heavy.

Jeff felt led to ask Tom a question. "Did your dad ever tell you what the war was like?"

Tom looked down at the bunch of dried flowers on the bench beside him. "In his letters, my dad was very honest. He told my mom details."

Jeff pressed on. "What did he say?"

"He talked a lot about the horrible insects." Tom took a deep breath. "I still remember his words. He called them the incredible, flying, crawling, slithering, stinging, biting, chewing, blood-sucking insects, bugs, slugs, leeches, and varmints of Vietnam."

"You remember detail like that?"

"I've read his letters hundreds of time. I almost feel like I know my dad from reading them."

Jeff sensed that this was helping Tom. "What else?" he asked.

"He wrote of the sounds of war—the horrible hiss of an incoming mortar round. Then there was the mud. Just look at the shore. He called it boot-sucking mud that added ten pounds to each foot, every step you took."

By now, Mindy and K.J. were captivated, too. K.J. had the video running.

"What else, Tom?" Jeff pressed.

"My dad talked about the mind-numbing boredom of walking up and down those endless hills following the green-clad, sweat-soaked back of the Marine in front of him. He talked about the sounds of the rock ape and the roar of tigers on faraway mountaintops."

Mindy's eyes got big. "You did say on some faraway mountaintop, didn't you?"

"The funny thing is," Tom said, "it wasn't tigers they feared. The war forced them to fear people. The thing my dad talked about the most was the close relationships he had with some of the other soldiers. That's why he wrote so much about Lloyd. He was a Christian, too, and they would pray together to make it through another day."

The boat pulled ashore with a thud. The strange men were still quite a ways down the river. Jeff prayed they would just pass by.

Cheng gave instructions to the boat driver. The plan was to allow Tom to spend a few hours here. There was no grave to mark the place where his father had died, but he would leave the dried flowers in his memory.

Making their way along the shore was slow work. Jeff peered into the jungle. The midday sun was unbearable. Wiping sweat from his forehead with the sleeve of his shirt, he wished he could duck under the dense foliage for some shade. But he knew Tom was on a mission.

Cheng looked at his map. "This is the general area."

Jeff walked beside Tom, just behind Mindy and Cheng. Tom had given K.J. permission to videotape the first moments of this visit. Everyone walked slowly, sensitive to Tom's feelings. Later, Jeff would do the interview. Now was the time for Tom to weep and grieve.

Cheng stopped walking. Tears filled his eyes. "In this area, so many soldiers lost their lives."

Hearing this, Tom sank to his knees, sobbing.

Chapter 11

Robbed

Knowing Tom needed to be alone, the others let him be. Jeff couldn't imagine what emotions Tom must be feeling as he stood a few hundred feet from where his dad must have died.

Jeff was relieved that the men had kept on going and hadn't stopped to harass them. He decided they must have been satisfied just to get pictures of the team—satisfied for now at least.

K.J. got Cheng to help him videotape the river and the jungle around them. Jeff and Mindy found a clearing to rest in about fifty feet away.

"This hasn't been an easy trip, has it?" Jeff said.

Mindy began to cry. "I feel so bad for Tom. I can't imagine what it would be like. I love Daddy so much, and Tom lost his dad when he was only five."

"And he saw him last when he was four, when his dad was home for the last time."

Mindy wiped her eyes. "What do people do who don't have the Lord? What about all the Vietnamese families who lost their loved ones? Many of them were Buddhists who believe people come back in another life. We only have one life. They need God."

Jeff put his arm around his sister. Her love for the Vietnamese people was deepening.

"So many people say the war was a waste," Mindy said, "and I don't know if it was or not. I just know God can bring good out of it now."

"I think so, too," Jeff agreed. "I think it's one of the reasons He sent us. He wants us to get people praying back home and to send more people back here, if for no other reason than to love these hurting people and get rid of the hate between us."

"The Vietnamese have always wanted their freedom," Mindy said. "I wish they all knew that only Jesus can give them real freedom."

For the next couple of hours, Cheng, Mindy, K.J., and Jeff talked about ways to reach Vietnam. Tom walked around quietly, dealing with his memories.

When he was ready, Tom found them down by the river.

Jeff looked at his smiling face. "Boy, you sure look happy."

Tom nodded back at the jungle. "I've come to a new peace about my dad's death. God gave me a strong impression of what a special man my dad was, a true hero. Whether the whole war was right or not, he died fighting for freedom."

❖❖❖❖❖❖❖

It was almost nine p.m. when Cheng pulled the van into the compound.

"I'm beat," Mindy cried. "I'm going to check on Warren, put a few things in my computer, and go to bed."

Jeff felt proud of his sister and the things she had shared earlier in the day.

Mindy headed inside.

K.J. was still going strong. "Do you think I should bring some extra light tomorrow? I want to get some good shots in the tunnels."

Jeff shrugged. "You're the ace cameraman. All I know is we need to check on Warren. I'll bet he's better after sleeping all day."

Jeff, Cheng, and K.J. carried the bags of equipment inside.

No one was in the living room, so they headed for the bedroom. Warren was sitting up in bed, looking sweaty and feverish. Mindy stood at his side.

"How you doing?" Jeff asked.

"Better. But I'm afraid I might need one more day in bed."

"We need to get you to a doctor," Mindy insisted.

Warren sat up straighter. "I'm really much better. One of the staff got me some medicine. I should be ready for Hanoi."

Everyone smiled knowingly. Warren was a rugged traveler, and unless he thought it was serious, he refused to make a big deal over picking up bugs.

"Okay," Mindy surrendered. "But if you're not doing better in the morning..."

Warren grinned. Mindy tossed him another pillow to put behind his back and took off for her room. While Cheng went to check phone messages, Tom, Jeff, and K.J. reported to Warren about the day.

Suddenly, a scream filled the house. It was coming from Mindy's room. With a shot of adrenaline, Jeff leaped up. Terrified, he ran into her room.

Mindy was just sitting on the edge of the bed.

"What's wrong?" he cried.

"My laptop. It's been stolen."

Jeff stared at his sister in disbelief. "Are you sure?"

Tears spilled out from behind Mindy's glasses. "I knew I shouldn't have left it here, but I didn't want to take it on the boat or leave it in the van, either."

By now everyone was in the room.

"Her computer's gone," Jeff explained.

Warren walked over to the desk where Mindy had been pointing. "Are you sure that's where it was?"

"Look, you guys. I'm not making this up. It's gone. Totally GONE. GONE!

Still weak, Warren sat down on the red overstuffed chair by Mindy's window.

"Who would have known it was here?" K.J. asked.

The only people Jeff could think of were staff members, and he couldn't bear to think any of them would steal it. He didn't think they'd even use it without permission.

Cheng looked troubled. "We've never had a theft

in the three years we've lived here. If the staff members aren't aware of anything, I'll call the police and see if they'll come out."

"With staff coming and going, it's possible a door got left open or unlocked," Warren said.

"Very possible," Cheng agreed. "Someone could even have taken a screen out of an open window."

Jeff went and sat beside Mindy.

"All of my research stuff was on it. My diary and our schedule. Everything."

"Didn't you back it up?" K.J. asked.

"Of course!" Mindy snapped. "Everything is backed up on disks at home, and I..."

Mindy jumped up from the bed and went to look through a bag in the closet. "Thank God. It's here." She held up the computer disk. "I just backed everything up last night before I went to bed. But I don't have anything to play it on."

"You can use my computer if it's compatible," Cheng said.

Mindy tried to smile.

"You still have it insured, don't you?" Warren asked.

"Yeah. My parents have always had it on their policy. It's just that I loved *that* computer."

"You'll get a better one," K.J. said.

"It's not the same," Mindy fumed. "What if it were your camera?"

Jeff stood up. "I know you're upset, but getting mad at the people trying to help you won't get your computer back."

"Sorry, K.J.," Mindy said. "You didn't hear anything, Warren?"

Warren shook his head, his face pale against the red fabric of the chair. "I was so sick, I slept most of the day."

By the time the police arrived to take a report, everyone was exhausted. When they were gone, Jeff climbed into bed with mixed emotions. Tom had had an incredible day of healing, and that was the most important thing. But he still felt bad for Mindy. He couldn't figure how the theft had happened. None of the staff members had seen anything. And he couldn't believe the red tape involved with telling the police the story. Everyone had gone over every detail three or four times, and the police still looked at everyone with suspicion, as if the whole story were just made up.

The next morning, Warren was giving Jeff instructions for their day at the tunnels when someone pounded on the bedroom door.

"Come in," Warren called.

Cheng burst in carrying a newspaper. He laid it flat on Jeff's bed. "Look at this."

Jeff looked down. All he could see was Vietnamese writing. Cheng laughed nervously, realizing Jeff couldn't read it.

"What is it?" Jeff cried.

"Le Duc has written another story."

Chapter 12

Deadly Hideout

Jeff groaned. "What kind of lies are in this one?"

"He's just expanding on the lies he already told. It seems he knows a lot about you. Tom must have told him everything. The article talks about the club and our trip to the Mekong Delta. It even mentions that we're going to Hanoi."

"How would he know that?" Warren asked.

Something clicked in Jeff's mind. "It actually makes sense," he said.

Cheng was surprised. "It does?"

"Yeah. Maybe those guys on the river worked for him, like you said. And I wouldn't be surprised if Le

Duc stole Mindy's computer. That could be how he's getting inside information."

"But how would he know Mindy even had a computer?" Warren asked.

"Who knows?" Jeff said. "Maybe Tom talked about it at the bar. Or maybe Le Duc's had people spying on us when we haven't noticed. I never would have noticed the men who followed us to the delta if I hadn't seen them on the dock."

"It makes more sense than anything I've thought of yet," Warren admitted. "Why don't you get the others, and we'll all talk about it."

Jeff quickly gathered everybody into the bedroom. Cheng read the article.

"So what do we do now?" K.J. asked. "This guy is dragging our reputation through the slimy mud. Pretty soon, everybody will believe him."

"And since the article says we're Christians, all the lies are hurting God's reputation, too," Mindy said.

Tom looked upset. "That's the worst part."

They were all quiet for a moment.

"I know," Jeff said suddenly. "If we could prove he's responsible for stealing Mindy's computer, his career might be over."

"He's not dumb enough to leave her computer lying around," K.J. said.

"But he might keep a computer disk in his office," Mindy countered.

Cheng smiled. "You Americans make good investigators."

Jeff pressed his idea. "Let's have Cheng call the police—tell them what we suspect. It may take a while, but they could run into something. Then we'll be vindicated."

"Le Duc probably has the police in his back pocket," Warren pointed out.

"You're probably right," Cheng said. "But things are pretty unpredictable here. The police may go for it."

Mindy's eyes lit up. "Why don't we call Donny, our guardian angel reporter? Other reporters like to get hot stories. Maybe he'll do some snooping around."

Warren nodded, affirming the idea. "If Cheng is willing, great. But let's keep our goals for this trip first in our minds, and not the enemy."

Jeff nodded. He knew from past experience how important that was.

"What time are we leaving for the tunnels?" K.J. asked. "It's after nine already."

Jeff looked at Cheng. He knew K.J. had been looking forward to filming the tunnels for a long time.

"An hour would give me time to make the phone calls," Cheng said. "Why don't we leave by ten?"

❖ ❖ ❖ ❖ ❖ ❖ ❖

Jeff was getting tired of sitting in planes and cars, but he was definitely thankful to be riding in the huge van. Camera equipment, a cooler of lunches, and extra sweatshirts in case the tunnels were cold sat on the spare seats. On most of their trips, the team rode buses and took taxis. Fitting everyone and their equipment into a taxi made for some crowded rides.

"Can you tell us about the tunnels?" Mindy asked.

"Sure," Cheng said. "They're one of Vietnam's biggest tourist attractions, especially since the entrance is less than an hour from Saigon."

"What makes them such a big attraction?" K.J. asked.

Cheng slowed down, turning onto a narrow street. "The North survived the war because of them. It's an astonishing complex of underground tunnels extending for miles. Many of them are three levels and as deep as twenty meters."

K.J. looked confused.

Mindy jumped in. "That's about sixty or seventy feet."

"Wow," K.J. gasped.

"Some of them were big enough to hold conference halls, food storage, work areas, hospitals, and even kitchens with vents that led to smoke outlets several hundred yards away."

"So nobody could see the smoke," K.J. said.

Cheng nodded. "Right. The Americans tried all sorts of experiments, including bombs, to drive the Communists out of the tunnels, but they never succeeded."

"Why not?" Jeff asked.

"Because the tunnel compartments were separated by trap doors that sealed the sections off from one another."

"That was smart," K.J. said. "The whole thing was smart."

Jeff was intrigued by the tunnels, too, but he kept remembering that they had been built for war, to kill and to escape from killing. "Does visiting these places bother you, Tom?"

"I'm okay," Tom said. "Don't worry. Some of these things aren't easy, but God is in my heart now. That makes all the difference."

"Amen," Cheng said.

"I thought I read something about U.S. bombers destroying the tunnels," Mindy said.

Cheng shook his head. "That's only partially true. It wasn't until the end of the war that the Americans sent in B-52 bombers to level the whole place. These tunnels we're visiting survived all that. There were a lot more." Cheng pulled into a parking lot.

"How long are these?" K.J. asked.

"About 125 miles."

"What level did the soldiers stay on?"

Cheng grinned. "You sure are full of questions. Usually, everyone stayed on the upper level. In times of danger, they dove to the second and third levels through shafts big enough to handle a thin Vietnamese."

Mindy laughed. "That would give you a good reason to watch your diet."

Jeff was surprised by how many cars were in the parking lot. After parking the van, Cheng led them past the visitor center, directly to the entrance. They walked through an open shaft and down some steps into the tunnels. K.J. began filming immediately.

Jeff was astonished. The dirty tunnels got wide, then narrow, then wide again. Some were high, others low. They went on and on. They were more incredible than Cheng had described. Lots of people were milling around. Jeff hoped that the Vietnamese tourists hadn't seen any Saigon newspapers.

Jeff took a slow, deep breath. "It's hard to breathe down here."

Cheng laughed. "Sorry. We Vietnamese need less air than you."

Jeff laughed, knowing he was joking.

"How long did people live here?" Mindy asked.

"For months at a time. Children were even born here. Sometimes the Americans filled the tunnels with poison gas. But the Vietnamese would wriggle on their hands and knees until they came to a well. They would survive under water for hours at a time by breathing through a reed."

They followed the tunnel branches in amazement. Cheng translated the information signs as they went.

By three o'clock, Jeff was ready to go. "How long do you guys want to stay here?"

"I'm ready to go if everyone else is," Mindy said. "I'm hungry. We never did break for lunch."

Everyone agreed that they should go. As they headed for the main entrance, Jeff spotted two familiar faces. He hung back until he was walking next to Cheng.

"It's the guys who followed us on the river," he whispered.

Cheng stopped walking. "Everyone turn around calmly and go back inside. We need to hide for a few minutes."

"We'll see if these tunnels really work," K.J. muttered.

They followed Cheng away from the entrance.

Cheng looked back, breathing fast. "Let's go this direction until it's clear."

"How will we know that?" Mindy asked.

"I don't know. We'll just have to follow our senses."

Cheng led them deeper into the tunnels, turning and turning until Jeff lost all sense of direction. Finally, he stopped, settling on a remote section of the tunnels to hide. Very few tourists were in this deep.

"Boy," K.J. laughed. "I'm starting to get the idea of how these guys must have felt when they were chased. Maybe we should go down to the next level."

Mindy shivered. "Very funny."

Jeff paced the tunnel, ten steps deeper and ten steps back. Nervously, they waited, first five minutes, then ten, then fifteen.

"I think it's safe to go," Cheng said.

They walked cautiously back the way they had come. By the time they got near the entrance, they were feeling confident. Then Jeff felt the short hairs on the back of his neck tingle. Four men holding wooden clubs were right in front of them, blocking their next turn.

Chapter 13

Hanoi

Tom let out a gasp. "It's Le Duc."

Jeff felt like flattening himself against the tunnel wall. He had always wanted to meet Le Duc, but not in a cave. Not trapped by thugs with clubs. Everyone stood perfectly still. Jeff sent up a quick, desperate prayer. Cheng had been right about the river men working with Le Duc.

Le Duc laughed. "I've finally got you trapped, Mr. Douglas."

Hearing him speak clear English gave Jeff the chills. He couldn't take his eyes away from Le Duc's left hand. It was in a splint. It looked like his finger had been broken.

Cheng said something in Vietnamese. The men didn't answer.

Jeff felt a boldness come over him. "What is it you want?" he asked. "Tom has apologized. Why don't you leave us alone?"

Le Duc moved closer until he was leaning in Jeff's face. "I hate you Americans. Especially your friend Tom." He held up his left hand and shook it at Tom. "You're going to pay for this."

Jeff felt the man's anger build. The three men stood behind him, each holding a club.

Le Duc's stare was cold. "I'm so glad we defeated you in the war. But I still hate what you did to our country."

Mindy tried another approach. "Tom came here to grieve for his father. We also grieve for the Vietnamese who died, people like Cheng's father and maybe some of your relatives, too."

Le Duc smirked. "I have no pity for Tom's father or any American. I wish we could have killed more."

The hatred in these words shocked Jeff. He knew Le Duc was bound by deep rage and bitterness. Cheng was obviously frightened. Mindy was shaking noticeably. K.J. held his camera at his side, against his leg. He looked relaxed, but Jeff knew better. Suddenly, Jeff realized that the red record light was on. K.J. was recording what they were saying.

Jeff followed Le Duc's gaze to the red light.

Le Duc put out his hand. "Okay, kid. Give me the tape."

Trembling, K.J. slipped the tape out of the camcorder and tossed it to him.

A security guard walked down the main tunnel calling out something in Vietnamese.

"What's he saying?" Jeff whispered. "Maybe he can help us."

"He's telling us all it's closing time."

Instantly, Jeff was hit with an idea. He doubled over, groaning like he was sick. "I can't breathe," he cried. "I can't breathe."

The security guard had passed their tunnel, but he ran back when he heard Jeff. The men held their clubs behind their backs.

"I can't breathe," Jeff cried again.

"Help us," Cheng pleaded. "He needs fresh air in a hurry."

The security guard ushered them half-running to the entrance. Outside, everyone ran full speed for the van. Cheng fumbled with the lock on the side door. They all piled in, locking the door behind them. Cheng sped away. Looking back, they could see Le Duc and his men standing at the entrance, watching.

"I want to go back for my tape," K.J. said as the men faded from view. "I had some great footage on there."

Mindy reached for the cooler of lunches. "What was it?"

"All the footage from the tunnels. I changed the tape this morning, or it would have been worse. We'll have to come again to get more footage."

Mindy tossed him a sandwich. "I don't think so. You can go back if you want to. It would take the whole Vietnamese army to get me back there."

Everyone laughed.

"If I went back," Jeff said, "I'd expect Le Duc around every corner."

Jeff was glad when they finally pulled into the compound. Warren listened almost in disbelief to their story. He was sitting in the living room, looking much better.

"You're going to Hanoi, aren't you?" Mindy asked.

"I think so. By morning, I should feel as good as ever. It's too bad they took the tape. We could have put an end to this tonight."

Jeff frowned. "I don't think we'll be seeing that tape any time soon."

As the team prepared to board their six a.m. flight, Jeff felt strangely nervous. He couldn't stop thinking about how crazy Le Duc had been in the tunnels. Leaving Ho Chi Minh City for a couple of days was probably a good idea.

Taking the two-hour flight on Vietnam Airlines into Hanoi wasn't in their original plan, but Jeff had learned on previous adventures to be flexible. By the time the plane landed in Hanoi, he had relaxed almost completely. As the plane taxied down the runway toward their gate, he couldn't help but notice the bomb craters around the airport. He began to think that their trip would have been incomplete without visiting the North.

The taxi ride to downtown Hanoi went slowly. Warren and Cheng talked in the front seat. Jeff sat squeezed in with Tom, Mindy, and K.J. in the back. He watched the countryside as the taxi driver bullied his way through the stream of traffic on the bumpy road. The men he saw wore plain black trousers with tightly buttoned white jackets. The women wore long coatlike garments over plain black trousers. This was very different from the variety of clothing he had seen in Ho Chi Minh City.

The traffic came to a sudden stop. The road was being repaired. K.J. leaned out the window to film. Jeff couldn't believe his eyes. A pair of oxen stood in the road, hitched with steel spikes to a bottomless wooden cart. Suspended in the cart was what looked like an old oil tank. A smokestack jutted from the top of the tank. A big grill underneath the tank held a fire fed by large branches.

"The fire's heating the tar in that tank," Cheng explained.

Jeff held his nose. The tar stunk to high heaven. Twenty minutes later, traffic thinned and the taxi squeezed through.

Jeff looked at Mindy when there was a lull in the conversation. "Why don't you give us a research report?"

Mindy grinned. "I was just watching the people work in the fields. I remember learning that there are four main types of work in Vietnam, the woodcutter, the fisherman, the farmer, and the herdsman. So far, we've seen all of them but the woodcutter."

Jeff nodded. He spotted some bridges Cheng had told them about. All around them were wide, flat rice paddies cut by dams into thousands of small plots. Black water buffalo pulled heavy hand-carved plows and rakes through the mud. Thin, sinewy farmers dressed in straw hats and dark clothes walked behind their buffalo in the thigh-deep mud, guiding them. Jeff remembered seeing pictures of North Vietnamese people during the war, all dressed alike.

"What did these farmers do during the bombings?" Tom asked.

"A siren sounded, and they fled to air-raid shelters," Cheng said.

"There are your woodcutters, Mindy." Jeff pointed to some men with axes chopping felled trees into smaller pieces.

"What bridge is that?" K.J. asked, pointing ahead.

Cheng grinned. "An important one. It crosses the Red River into Hanoi."

Once they were across the bridge, Jeff saw the city. It reminded him of the architecture he had seen when he studied France in school. As they drove through it, he was amazed. He had expected Hanoi to be scarred by the American bombing. It wasn't. Many of its buildings were run down and needed repair though. Jeff looked past the dirt and saw the city's beautiful architecture and graceful landscaping. Trees lined the avenues and streets, and they drove past several well-tended public parks and gardens. Workers were repairing the old, cracked stucco buildings. Teams of women wearing kerchiefs over their mouths were filling potholes in the streets, pulling carts of tar and sand behind them. Hundreds of bicycles were on the road, just like in Saigon.

The taxi pulled up in front of a hotel.

"First, we'll check in," Cheng said. "Then we'll go look up Mr. Lang's friend."

Inside, Jeff studied the small lobby. Except for the smiling faces of the employees, the hotel was nothing like the one in Bangkok. From cracked cement, crumbling mortar, and sagging windows outside, to faded and peeling paint inside, the place was desperately in need of repair.

"I hope you don't mind," Cheng said. "I didn't want to spend too much money."

"It's fine," Warren assured him. "We don't have a lot of extra money to spend."

When Cheng had filled out the check-in paperwork, they went to their rooms. The first thing Jeff noticed was the sound of a giant air conditioner laboring in the window. He moved closer, expecting a mighty blast of cold air. For all the noise, the room was only a little cooler than the tropics outside. The walls were covered with mildew, and the windows were black with soot. The bathroom was lined with cracked tiles.

"How long are we staying?" Mindy asked, coming over from her room.

"Hopefully only a day," Cheng said. "If we have to, we can change hotels. There are a couple of things I want to show you in the city if we have the time."

K.J. grinned. "We have the time. And I've got my camera ready."

Later that day, they took a taxi to the apartment building of Mr. Lang's friend. Jeff felt relieved to be out of Ho Chi Minh City. All he wanted was a calm Thursday.

The taxi driver stopped in front of an old apartment complex. It needed repair, but it was in better
shape than their hotel. Tom was the first one out of
the taxi. Jeff scrambled out after him. Scanning the
piece of paper in Cheng's hand, Jeff saw that the
man's name was Van Quang. He prayed this wasn't
a wild goose chase.

"Let's see if this guy is home," K.J. said. He had
his camera bag with him because it didn't seem
safe to leave it in their hotel room. Warren had
made it clear, though, that he wasn't to film on this
visit.

Everyone followed Cheng and Warren up the
stairs. Cheng knocked. Finally, the door opened. A
large Vietnamese man with dark features and black,
tinted glasses filled the tiny doorway. A scraggly
mustache dominated his face. He said something in
Vietnamese, revealing a deep, hoarse voice.

Cheng spoke with him for a moment. Everyone
waited to hear what had been said. Tom leaned in
with anticipation. Finally, Mr. Quang spoke English
and invited everyone inside. Jeff was surprised.

The man showed them to the living room.
"Please sit down," he said. "Mr. Lang told me you
might be coming. I'm glad you decided to let me
help you."

"We hear you have proof that Lloyd Thompson
is alive," Tom said.

"I do."

"Can you show us the proof?"

"Certainly." Mr. Quang pulled out some pictures
from a nearby briefcase. "These were taken six
months ago. My sources tell me he has been spotted

north of Hanoi in some kind of work camp."

Jeff felt suspicious. "Can we look at those pictures?"

Mr. Quang handed them to him. Jeff gave them to Tom.

Tom studied the man. "I'm not sure. He's definitely an American. I saw pictures my dad sent us of Lloyd. It kinda looks like him. I'm just not sure."

"We must be absolutely sure," Jeff said. "This whole thing could be a hoax."

Mr. Quang's face turned red. "Look kid. I don't have time to waste. If you're not interested in helping free this man, there's the door."

Jeff chewed on his lip, not liking what he felt.

"Just a minute," Tom said. "I'm interested. I owe it to my dad to take the chance."

"Is there any other proof that would help Tom identify him?" Warren asked.

Mr. Quang pulled out two more pictures. "These might interest you. Have a look." He handed them to Tom. Jeff and the others moved in closer.

"It's a picture of dog tags," Tom said. "Look. His name is on them."

Jeff looked at the pair of metal tags strung on a chain.

"Dog tags are a soldier's identification tags," K.J. said. "Like you put on a dog."

"We know that, K.J.," Mindy said softly. "Everybody knows that."

K.J. blushed.

"And here's another picture of him," Tom said. "I can't be sure about the man, but these are his dog tags."

Tom looked directly at Mr. Quang. "How much would you charge to take us to him?"

Mr. Quang did some quick figuring on a piece of paper. "One thousand dollars."

Chapter 14

Pressure Building

Everyone looked shocked. Jeff was ready to leave, but he knew Tom was not. Silence filled the room. All they could do was look at each other. And wait.

Tom took a deep breath. "Why does it cost so much?"

"Because it's dangerous. The government doesn't like us snooping around. Vietnam has better relations with America now. News of finding soldiers alive only stirs up the American people. Also, if your government found out you were looking for Mr. Thompson, they wouldn't be very happy. In fact, they have an office in Hanoi that works on that."

"Why don't we go to the office and find out ourselves then?" Mindy asked.

Tom's face stiffened. "I know families who have tried that. They never hear anything. The U.S. government is wrapped in red tape like everything else."

"What if we don't find him?" Warren asked. "Do we still have to pay?"

"I'll take six hundred up front and four hundred after we find him. If we don't locate him dead or alive, I'll give you half of the up-front money back. The rest is for expenses. If you want to, we can start early tomorrow morning. It's a two-hour drive. Then we'll hike up the hills. Rumor has it that they move these prisoners around. I can't guarantee anything."

Tom looked at Warren. "What do you think?"

"Why don't we talk it over? We can call Mr. Quang later, after we've had some time to think and pray about it."

Mr. Quang nodded. "You can talk it over. But I need an answer by three p.m. if you want to go tomorrow."

Jeff looked at his watch. It was close to one.

"Fair enough," Tom said. "We'll give you a call either way."

Outside, the team huddled together.

"I'm sure glad you're with us today," Jeff said.

Warren nodded, wiping sweat from his forehead. The North was supposed to be cooler, but the heat was nearly unbearable today. "This has to be Tom's decision since his uncle is paying. My job is to make sure it will be safe."

Tom traced a crack in the sidewalk with his toe. "I may never get back here. Even if Lloyd's not alive, if I could just find proof that he died, it'll bring peace to his family. My uncle told me to spend the money as I think my dad would want it spent."

"I see why you need to do this," Mindy said, "but I don't know if I can trust this guy. Why don't we go to that U.S. office and at least ask them about Lloyd?"

"That's not a bad idea," Jeff said. "We could take a taxi down there."

Cheng nodded. "I think we should give it a try. It may give us our answer."

"Are you willing, Tom?" Warren asked.

"As long as you don't all close your minds to Mr. Quang."

❖❖❖❖❖❖❖

Jeff was glad to see an American flag as the taxi stopped in front of an old looking building. The sign out front said, "United States Task Force-Full Accounting." Up the street, two peddlers dozed beside their fruit-laden baskets.

Everyone piled out as Warren paid the driver. Inside was the welcome sight of more American flags and familiar khaki uniforms. Tom walked up to the counter. The office looked just like Jeff thought a military office would—flags, khaki, and gray chairs and desks. He felt a little nervous.

An older officer with close-cropped hair and reading glasses stood up from his desk behind the counter. "May I help you?" he asked.

"My name is Tom Douglas..." Jeff listened as Tom explained everything he knew about Lloyd.

The officer nodded as if he had heard many similar stories. "Just a minute, sir. I'll check if we have anything new for you."

Moments later, the man returned. "I'm sorry, sir. Our records show that Lloyd Thompson is still reported as missing in action. I wish we could help."

Jeff felt his heart drop. He had been hoping for news that would give them an option other than Mr. Quang.

The officer's eyes were piercing. "We've had many family members visit Hanoi. We know you're desperate for information. But be careful. There are crooks who will give you phony stories for money."

Jeff exchanged nervous glances with Mindy.

Outside, the team stood on the street corner trying to decide what to do next.

Mindy knelt down to tie her shoe. "Did you hear what he said? It sounds a little risky."

Tom's eyes filled with intensity. "I don't think Mr. Quang is a crook. Those pictures are proof. What do we have to lose by checking it out? I'm paying for it."

K.J. laughed nervously. "Maybe our lives."

Jeff shuddered. With K.J., it was hard to tell when he was being dramatic and when he was really scared.

"We'll stand by you, Tom," Warren said. "You have to make the decision."

Tom went back and leaned against the stone wall of the corner building, deep in thought. Everyone waited quietly, praying.

A few minutes later, Tom's face hardened in determination. "Look. I've made a decision. I'll go alone and meet you guys back in Hanoi tomorrow night. I have to check it out."

"You're not going alone," Jeff protested. "I'll go with you."

"Well, you aren't leaving me behind," K.J. said. "This could be the greatest story of my life."

"Whether you find him or not," Mindy pointed out, "it'll be hard for you. It would be awful to be alone."

They all looked at Warren, knowing he would make the final decision about whether team members would go.

"It'll probably be safer if we all go," Warren decided. "This could be a wild goose chase, so we'll get specific information about where we're going. We'll let Cheng's staff in Saigon know everything we know."

"That's a good idea," Cheng agreed. "The more people who know, the better."

Tom smiled. His face was peaceful for the first time since talking with Mr. Quang. Jeff understood completely why he had to get an answer.

By the time Cheng found a phone and called Mr. Quang to make arrangements to go the next day, they had barely made the three o'clock deadline.

"So what are we going to do now?" Jeff asked. "We've got hours to kill, and there's nothing to do back at the hotel."

"I vote we get something to eat," K.J. said.

Cheng grinned. "I know a really good restaurant not far from here. Let's get some lunch. Then I'll show you some sights."

"What were you thinking?" Warren asked.

"First, I think you need to see the Hanoi Hilton. It's the prison where American soldiers were held."

"I've heard about that," K.J. said. "It'll work into the video really well if I can get some good shots."

"We can have a prayer meeting there," Mindy said. "We can pray for all the families who lost loved ones in the war."

"We could," Cheng said, smiling at Mindy. "I also have another surprise for you, but this time I won't hold you in suspense. I want you to see an orphanage run by my friend Mr. Cao. I called from Saigon to let him know we might stop by. Be prepared for your hearts to break. Mr. Cao's home is filled with kids who need love."

❖❖❖❖❖❖❖

After lunch, the team caught a taxi to the Hanoi Hilton.

Cheng pointed to the massive security walls towering above them. "Its real name is the Hoa Lo Prison. The POWs held here during the war are the ones who started calling it the Hilton. It's about as far as you can get from a fancy American hotel."

"They had to laugh about something," Warren said.

"Or go crazy," Tom agreed. "My dad wrote about the strange mix of humor and terror—men seeing something horrible one minute and laughing the next. He said it was the only way to cope sometimes."

"I'm surprised there's a prison in the center of the city," Mindy said.

Cheng nodded. "This is not the most popular part of town." Jeff followed Cheng's gaze to the run-down buildings, crumbling sidewalks, and littered streets. Raw sewage ran down the side of the road.

The stone walls of the prison were at least twenty feet high. Large shards of broken glass were embedded in a section of concrete at the top. The mass of sharp glass was more than a foot high. Above that were six strands of barbed wire.

"It must have been practically impossible to escape," Jeff said.

Cheng nodded. "That barbed wire is electrified, too."

K.J. was busy filming, a look of astonishment on his face. He turned the camera on Cheng. "Tell us more about the prison."

Cheng looked into the camera. "This is still an active prison. The French built it for that purpose. Before World War II, the prisoners were Vietnamese put here by the French. During World War II, the prisoners were Vietnamese and French put here by the Japanese. During the next conflict, the prisoners were again Vietnamese. And of course, during the war between the North and South, the prisoners were Americans."

Jeff imagined what it must have been like to be an American prisoner there, spending hours thinking of your family and home and the awful things you had seen.

K.J. studied the walls. "I wish I could get in there. It would make some amazing footage."

Tom looked up at the lethal shards of glass. "It's very possible that Lloyd spent some time here."

"You're right," Cheng said.

Everyone was silent.

"Why don't we have some prayer?" Mindy said softly. "This place makes me feel so sad."

For the next few moments, the team prayed. Tears flowed down Tom's cheeks.

After a while, Cheng broke away from the group to flag a taxi coming down the street. It was time to move on. At that moment, Jeff felt strangely afraid, just as he had when they were on the boat in the Mekong Delta. Looking down the street, he didn't like what he saw.

It was two of the men who had trapped them in the tunnel.

Chapter 15

Booby Trap

Jeff didn't want to tell anyone, but he knew he had to let the others know.

"Don't look now, but we're being followed again."

Instinctively, everyone turned to look. The taxi pulled up to the curb in front of them.

"Get in," Warren ordered. "Let's get out of here."

In the taxi, everyone sat in stunned silence.

Mindy found her voice first. "What do we do now? I can't believe those guys came all the way to Hanoi. What's their problem?"

"Le Duc wants some kind of revenge on Tom," Jeff said.

"And on us," K.J. reminded everyone.

"We can't let them get to us," Warren said from the front seat. "We'll have to make sure we're in safe places."

"Yeah. Like in the middle of the jungle with Mr. Quang."

"We'll need to let Mr. Quang know what's going on. We'll sneak out in the morning."

"Here we go again," Mindy moaned.

K.J. grinned. "That's what this club is all about. We love adventure."

"It's a good thing we do," Jeff said.

"Are we still going to the orphanage?" Mindy asked.

Cheng nodded. "I think that's probably the safest place we could go right now, as long as they don't follow us there. We wouldn't want to endanger the children."

Mindy looked horrified at the thought.

"I've been watching," K.J. said. "The last I saw them, they were standing on the sidewalk watching us drive away."

"That's the last I saw them, too," Tom said.

They all searched the cars around them.

Cheng was satisfied. "Looks like we lost them."

"Probably not for long," Mindy muttered.

❖❖❖❖❖❖❖

They were all excited when they arrived at the orphanage. They had seen so many Vietnamese children on this trip. Now they could finally spend some time with them.

Jeff looked over the property. A large white stucco building with a red tile roof was surrounded by grass. When Jeff heard the squeals and laughter of kids playing, he knew Mindy would love the evening.

"Are there many orphanages in Vietnam?" Mindy asked as they walked to the door.

"I'm afraid so. You'll find them from north to south. Like in many poor countries, kids are abandoned and have no other place to live."

Cheng knocked. An older man came to the door. From what Cheng had told them, Jeff knew the man had a very limited income. He was dressed in a stained, slightly torn jacket, black pants, and worn sandals.

Cheng smiled. "This is the director, Mr. Cao. He's a very special man." Cheng introduced everyone in English.

"It's so nice to meet you," Mr. Cao said. "Cheng said you might stop by. Let me show you around. My staff members are working other jobs this evening. Some were just here to help with supper. Others will be back at bedtime. It takes a while to get eighty children in bed, you know—of course, some are old enough to help themselves."

He led them to a courtyard filled with kids. Round-faced children came running toward the gate. Older ones looked at the team curiously. Most were barefoot, wearing different colored shirts and baggy, black pants. Several small children ran to Mr. Cao, dirty but brilliant smiles lighting up their faces.

"Can we play with them?" Mindy asked, kneeling down in front of a group of wide-eyed five-year-olds.

"Please," Mr. Cao said. "These kids need a lot more love than our small staff can give."

It was clear to Jeff that Mr. Cao loved the children under his care. He could tell that the children possessed little more than the clothing on their backs, but each of them looked healthy. When one of them smiled, the smile was priceless.

Mindy picked up a little girl who giggled when Mindy smiled at her. "I'd like to take her home with me."

Jeff thought for a moment about the video they were producing. Realizing how powerful pictures of the orphanage would be, he talked to K.J. about getting some shots. They could let people in America know about the children so they could possibly be adopted.

"Do you mind if we interview you?" Jeff asked the director.

"Not at all. But please don't mention that Christians run the orphanage. It would get us in trouble. Just talk about the children."

"What ages do you have here?" Jeff asked while K.J. ran the camera. "And how long do they stay with you?"

"We have children from ages two to sixteen. We try to find homes for them, but some of these children have lived here since they were very little. We show as much love as we can..."

The camera rolled as Jeff continued the interview. He was impressed with Mr. Cao's big heart. He had given his life to these homeless children. Even though he didn't have much to work with, he was giving them love.

Suddenly, little children surrounded K.J. Seeing him pan the camera right into their smiling, curious faces gave Jeff an idea. He reached into K.J.'s equipment bag and got out the Polaroid camera. Excited, he began to shoot pictures of the kids and let them watch their photographic image slowly appear before them. The kids stared at the changing pictures, pointing and laughing.

"It's a good thing we brought lots of film," Mindy said. She helped Jeff arrange the children in small groups so they could all get in a picture.

Jeff studied the faces of the kids. In his research on the war, he had learned about the thousands of kids made parentless by the war. Still other children were left behind at the end of the war by their American fathers—soldiers, sailors, airmen, and Marines. The children of the war were older now like Tom, but they had once been the same age as the children now in the orphanage. Jeff fought to control his emotions, wondering about the sad story behind each face, wishing each child could have a mother and father.

After a while, Mr. Cao led them through the living quarters. There were three main rooms that housed thirty children each. Old metal bunk beds lined the walls, and toys lay sprawled on the concrete floors—rag dolls, wooden cars, bright plastic blocks. Rag rugs, some faded and some bright, were scattered on the floors. The odor of old mattresses and the outdoor toilets tainted the air. Jeff knew the smell would have been worse on a hotter day.

After the tour, Mr. Cao invited the team to stay for a while. Jeff watched with delight as Mindy played with the little kids and Warren, Tom, and Cheng talked with some of the older kids. Mr. Cao had explained that the oldest ones were out working or studying. At that moment, playing peekaboo with a yellow-shirted boy, Jeff wished he could help every kid in the world. But he knew he couldn't do it alone. It would take hundreds of workers worldwide who loved God and gave up their lives like Mr. Cao.

Jeff felt a deep sadness, thinking of how some of these children must be hurting. Mr. Cao had told them that some of the children were behind in their development or unable to accept love because of trauma and neglect. Sometimes the damage was permanent. Other times, nutrition, time, and love could heal them.

Jeff realized that the war had to affect even these kids, more than twenty years later. It had crippled their nation. He felt a deep disgust for war rising in his soul. He realized that war really was a tool of the devil for destruction. He knew that the design God created and intended was turned upside down by the powers of darkness. He knew it all began in the Garden of Eden when Adam and Eve fell into sin. Everything got messed up, and these kids were suffering from that rebellion. Jeff tried to imagine all the Vietnamese kids who had been killed by senseless bombings and booby traps. He remembered that Jesus was the Prince of Peace, the opposite of war.

Before Jeff knew it, K.J. had stopped filming and was playing with the kids. It was getting late, and they needed to get back to their hotel to prepare for the trip with Mr. Quang in the morning.

"How are we going to leave this place?" Mindy asked.

Jeff was wondering the same thing. "I don't know. I just know I'll be thinking about them for a long time."

"Me too," K.J. said. He put down a two-year-old boy squirming to get free. As soon as he did, the boy put his arms up and tugged at K.J.'s jeans. Laughing, K.J. picked him up again.

Warren gathered the team together. "It's time for us to go. Mr. Cao said staff members will be coming back soon to help him put the children to bed."

Reluctantly, Jeff said good-bye to Mr. Cao and the children. After lots of hugs and kisses, the team headed out into the cloudy evening.

Everyone felt nervous and excited at the same time as they rode in Mr. Quang's van the next morning. They had joined hands outside Mr. Quang's apartment, committing the trip to God and asking for His protection. Mr. Quang hadn't said much since getting in the van. Warren tried to make conversation, but Mr. Quang seemed deep in thought. All he gave were one-word answers. Jeff couldn't stop thinking about the money Tom had counted out back at the apartment. He hoped it would pay off.

As they headed north toward Langson, Jeff studied the landscape. No one seemed to feel much like talking. Jeff saw broken-down bridges and what looked like the faded brick remnants of French forts and bunkers built into the hilltops years ago. Carts, trucks, and bicycles, all loaded with pigs, chickens, and ducks, stirred up dust on the sides of the highway. Many of the animals were dead. Others were alive and tied together with ropes. The new green rice rose high, some of it ready for harvest. On the dirt roadside, women peddled baskets of pineapples, coconuts, and breadfruit.

Two hours passed before they went through a small town.

Mr. Quang looked over at Tom. "We'll park here and hike up that mountain aways. Wait here while I get some water and supplies."

Tom nodded. Everyone waited in the car except Cheng, who headed toward the little store nearby. Jeff figured he needed something.

Looking at his watch, he couldn't believe the date. "You guys won't believe it, but it's the Fourth of July."

"We'll miss all the fireworks," Mindy said.

"Maybe not," K.J. laughed.

Jeff was glad that the foothills of the mountain weren't very steep. He took a deep breath, hardly believing he was hiking into a Vietnamese jungle in search of a prison camp. Jeff tried to look ahead, but all he could see was more green jungle. Palm trees and thick bush grew closer and closer together the farther they walked. He could see that it might be easy to hide people in Vietnam.

Jeff was still trying to figure out Mr. Quang. Whenever he tried to start a conversation, Mr. Quang just grunted back a few words. It drove Jeff crazy.

"We don't have much farther," Mr. Quang said finally. "We'll need to be quiet. I'm told the camp is in a clearing just beyond those palms."

Jeff looked at Tom hiking up at the front of the group. Tom had been through so much already on this trip. Jeff really hoped he would find an answer for Lloyd's family. Moving closer to the cluster of large, thick palm trees, he uttered a quick prayer to God. He couldn't bear for Tom to be disappointed.

Jeff wiped the sweat dripping from his forehead. It was cooler than Ho Chi Minh City, but it was still hot. His hair was damp in the humidity. Finally they stood on the edge of the clearing. There was only one layer of trees between them and the camp. Everyone got quiet. Jeff held his breath, trying to imagine an American soldier surviving this long, trapped and dead to the world. Jeff had read of prison camps out in the Vietnam bush. Maybe Lloyd Thompson was held nearby.

Mr. Quang turned suddenly to face the team. He was holding a large black gun at his side. Jeff thought was a revolver. They all stared at Mr. Quang in shock. Were they going to have to kill a guard to get into the camp? That wasn't what they wanted at all.

Mr. Quang laughed. He brought the gun up. He pointed it at the team.

Chapter 16

The Danger Zone

Jeff screamed. The revolver's cylindrical cartridge chamber glistened green, reflecting the color of the jungle.

"I'm sorry to disappoint you, Mr. Douglas," Mr. Quang laughed. "But you've led your friends right into my trap."

Tom's face fell as if he had been hit with ten sledge hammers. K.J.'s eyes almost popped out of his head. Jeff felt as if he were in the middle of a nightmare. Confused, he agonized, trying to figure out why Mr. Quang was doing this. Was it money? Hate? He felt a sick feeling rise in the pit of his stomach.

Mr. Quang swung the revolver around wildly. "Quickly, behind those trees."

The team stumbled into the clearing. Jeff knew they were helpless. They were surrounded completely by thick jungle. He looked at Warren in horror. A huge bamboo cage rested unevenly on the brushy ground. Old and weatherworn, it was made of eight-inch bamboo stalks tied together with leather straps. The cage was taller than Jeff. Jeff stared at it, knowing exactly what it was. Like cages for wild animals, similar ones had been used to imprison American soldiers until they were killed or taken to the Hanoi Hilton. This cage would have been big enough for five to ten men.

Jeff felt Mr. Quang's hand on his back pushing him toward the cage. A door made of the same bamboo crossbars hung open on leather hinges.

"Get in," Mr. Quang ordered. "All of you."

He stood behind the team, training his gun on their backs. The team tripped over each other in their rush to cross the small clearing.

"Hurry up," he shouted.

Mindy reached the cage first. Jeff stumbled in behind Cheng.

"Pull the door shut," Mr. Quang ordered.

K.J. was standing by the open door frame. Warren nodded for him to do as he was told.

Mr. Quang laughed. "Thanks for helping me lock you in." With his left hand, he reached into the cloth bag around his neck and pulled out a chain and padlock. Jeff wondered how he was going to put it on with one hand.

"You," Mr. Quàng said, waving his gun at

Mindy. "Wrap this around here and pull it tight." He motioned to a bamboo stalk on the edge of the door and to one on the cage. Shaking, Mindy obeyed. She lined two links up on top of each other and let the excess chain hang down. Mr. Quang slipped a padlock through the two links and clicked the lock shut. Only then did he lower his gun.

He pulled out a cigarette and lighter. "Sit down. And if you talk, talk so I can hear you."

Mindy flinched at his gruff voice.

"Relax, little girl. You'll be staying here a while."

Mr. Quang paced in front of the cage for several minutes, then squatted down a few feet away. He laid the revolver on the ground in front of him.

Moments passed like hours. At first, everyone sat absolutely still, scared and in shock. Jeff looked up at the blue sky, then at the thick bamboo, thinking of the thousands of soldiers who had experienced this. He wondered what had gone through their minds as they pondered their cruel fate. Maybe they even stared out toward other cages filled with other prisoners of war. Jeff felt totally helpless.

"How could I have been so dumb?" Tom moaned.

"We all saw the dog tags," Mindy whispered. "We all fell for it."

"Speak up," Mr. Quang demanded, picking up his gun. "I can't hear you. You, Mr. Douglas, repeat what you said."

"I apologized for getting them into this mess."

Mr. Quang pointed the gun at K.J. "Is that what he said?"

"Yes," K.J. squeaked.

"Really?"

"Yes."

"You're lying."

"I'm not, I promise," K.J. said.

"And what did the little girl say?"

"That it wasn't his fault."

Mr. Quang pointed the gun at Mindy. "Is that what you said?"

Mindy edged back to the far wall of the cage. "I said we all saw the dog tags. We all fell for it."

Mr. Quang lowered his gun. "Sweet girl, trying to make him feel better."

Mindy's eyes flashed.

Jeff began to wonder if they'd ever see their mom and dad again. His mind racing, he watched Mr. Quang smoke one cigarette after another. Was the man who gave them Quang's address working with him? Jeff wanted to ask Warren about the chances for a search if they didn't come back that night, but it was impossible with Mr. Quang so close. Two long hours passed. Mindy sat at the back of the cage, hugging her knees.

Suddenly, Jeff was aware of voices coming up the mountain. Could this be help? Could this be a miracle? Everyone looked at Cheng. Cheng strained to hear, but he shook his head. He couldn't make out any words. Mr. Quang stood up, his gun in his hand.

Three men broke into the clearing. Tom gasped. Jeff's hope vanished. It was Le Duc and his two companions—the same men who had been on the river and in the tunnel.

Shocked, they all scrambled to their feet. What was Le Duc doing here? What did he have to do with Mr. Quang? Did he arrange this whole thing? How many other people had he trapped? What did he do with them? Jeff felt ready to burst. They had been trapped like animals, and they didn't even know why.

Le Duc took the gun from Mr. Quang. "How do you feel now, Mr. Tom Douglas? It's too bad your father never tried out one of these. But I'm sure his friend did."

Tom gripped the cage.

Le Duc laughed. The others joined in.

"Where is Lloyd?" Tom pleaded, still holding to a dying hope.

"We don't know. The pictures were phony."

Tom slumped to the ground, his hands sliding down the bars of the cage.

"What do you want with us?" Mindy demanded.

Mr. Quang smiled, his lips spread thinly over his teeth. "Relax, little girl. You'll be fine if you do what we ask."

Jeff kicked the cage. "Don't call her little girl like that." He hated the way Mr. Quang talked to his sister.

"Both of you," Warren ordered, "sit down and don't say a word."

"That would be wise," Le Duc snarled.

"What is it that you want?" Warren asked. "You already have our money."

"We never have enough," Le Duc said. "I'm sure your relatives in America will be very glad to help us when they find out about your new home." Le Duc laughed. "If they comply, you'll be on your way to California. If they don't, your club has probably taken its last trip."

Jeff finally figured it out. Pure greed. Le Duc was just another common criminal, driven by the love of money. The Communist beliefs that he claimed to support meant nothing to him.

"What are we going to do?" K.J. whispered.

Mr. Quang spit on the ground. "Shut up, kid."

Fighting rising fear, Jeff prayed.

Le Duc handed Warren a notebook and a pencil. "Give this to the blond boy."

Warren handed them to Jeff.

"Write down everyone's phone number," Le Duc ordered, "or their closest relative's number—especially that kid with the camera's."

"What about mine?"

"We already have yours."

At that moment, Jeff remembered the computer. For security, Mindy had only their own phone number on the computer.

"How long are you going to keep us here?" Mindy cried.

"A few hours," Mr. Quang said.

Le Duc and the other men burst into laughter.

"Yeah," Le Duc said. "A few hours. After that we'll move you deeper into the jungle."

"How long really?" Mindy pressed.

Le Duc shrugged. "After that, it's up to your families. We'll keep you for weeks if we have to, months even if they're too stupid to pay fast."

K.J. looked hopeless. "What if my family doesn't have any money?"

"It's amazing what people can come up with."

"Haven't you ever been caught?" Jeff asked, passing Le Duc back his notebook.

Le Duc scowled. "Never. I don't hire men who

get caught. Usually, I let them handle the whole thing. They change their names, and we do it again." He stared at Tom. "This time I have a special interest in the case. "

Mr. Quang took a long drink from his water bottle. "Poor suckers," he laughed. "Parents of missing soldiers will pay anything to get their children back. But they're dead. They died in the war."

Jeff looked over at Tom sitting slouched against the front of the cage. All Jeff could do was signal his sorrow with his eyes.

They all looked at each another, as if trying to formulate a plan. But their gazes kept going back to the thick bamboo. It was hopeless.

"Maybe we can make some kind of deal with them," Jeff whispered. Maybe..." Suddenly, Jeff heard a faint noise in the sky. He thought he was imagining things.

"Do you guys hear that?" Warren whispered.

Everyone sat still, listening to the faraway sound. It sounded like the churning blades of a helicopter. The noise grew louder and closer. Le Duc and his men started yelling at each other in Vietnamese.

"What are they saying?" Jeff asked.

"Le Duc is accusing his men of messing everything up."

Jeff looked up, searching the skies. K.J. got his camera out and ready.

Suddenly, the helicopter was in sight above the jungle. Jeff started screaming.

"Shut up," Le Duc shouted. "And put that camera down." He pointed the revolver at the cage for the first time.

The helicopter circled above the palms, not yet

over the clearing. Jeff prayed the pilot wouldn't turn around and leave. Suddenly, the helicopter moved their way.

"I hope they're the good guys," K.J. cried.

"They have to be better than Quang and Le Duc," Mindy said.

"They see us," Jeff cried. "They see us."

Le Duc and his men started running down the mountain.

Jeff and the others waved frantically, sticking their hands through the top of the cage. K.J. and Mindy jumped up and down. In his excitement, K.J. forgot to hold the camera steady. Jeff's mind was in a state of total confusion. How would anyone know they were in trouble? Was this the government coming after them for snooping around? Was this more enemies?

The chopper dropped into the clearing, its blades whipping up a swirling wind. Dust churned everywhere, and twigs and grass flew through the air. Jeff choked on the dust, but he didn't care. He just wanted to be free from Le Duc. Three men who looked like Vietnamese soldiers jumped out of the chopper and ran toward them. A fourth man dressed in civilian clothes followed.

"It's Donny," Cheng cried. "I don't believe it. It's my friend from the newspaper. How did he know?"

"The guardian angel," Mindy cried. "He's here."

K.J. was filming everything carefully now.

Cheng pointed down the mountain. "The men went that way," he shouted above the chopper noise. "Four of them."

A soldier nodded. "We saw. Do you know how they're armed?"

"They have at least one gun. Le Duc was holding it—a revolver."

Two of the soldiers were already taking a few running steps across the clearing.

The first soldier waved them on. "Go after them like we planned. You know what to do."

Jeff was glad one soldier would stay with them. He felt safer that way. The soldier broke the padlock open, and the chain fell to the ground. Donny swung the bamboo door open. Cheng ran out first, yelling a greeting over the noise. Jeff wondered if the helicopter was waiting to lift them out of there.

Warren shook Donny's hand and introduced himself. "How did you know we were here?"

"I got Cheng's message about the computer. We found one of Mindy's computer disks in Le Duc's office. Cheng had said something about going to Hanoi to meet a contact who claimed to know about a prison camp. I called the compound to see if someone there knew how to get a hold of you so I could tell you about the computer. They sounded worried about you going with Mr. Quang into the jungle, so I investigated it. When I realized that Mr. Quang's operation fit the description of complaints from other families who had been swindled, I knew you were in trouble. What I wasn't sure of was whether Le Duc had anything to do with it."

"That's because he usually leaves all the dirty work to his men," Cheng said. "He doesn't have any contact with his victims. He just shares in the profit."

"That sounds like him," Donny said.

"How did you know where to look for us?" Mindy asked.

"Cheng made a phone call to his staff and told them your general location. It probably saved your lives."

Jeff remembered Cheng going to the little store.

"I knew Cheng called," Warren said, "but I had no reason to think anyone would be looking for us until tomorrow. By then, Le Duc could have moved us far into the jungle."

Tom raised his arms in thanksgiving. "This is the second time someone's saved me."

❖❖❖❖❖❖❖

At the bottom of the hill, a van waited to take Jeff and the others back. Le Duc, Mr. Quang, and the other two men were sitting in a Vietnamese prison wagon. Jeff knew they wouldn't be doing business for a long time.

Donny stood next to Cheng. "I'm going to write a new article. You guys will be Vietnamese heroes soon."

Warren smiled at him.

"Not only that," Donny added. "The police have Mindy's computer, and it's in perfect shape."

Mindy ran over to hug him. Everyone laughed.

"Have we had enough fireworks for the Fourth of July?" Jeff teased.

"More than enough," Mindy grinned.

K.J. held up his camera. "And it isn't over yet. I still have some footage to shoot. And more interviews. This could be my best story ever. What I've found out is that I love Vietnam."

"Me too," Tom said, smiling at Cheng and Donny.

"I'm sorry I fell for this dumb scheme, you guys. I put you all in danger following Mr. Quang."

Jeff looked him in the eye. "I'm real sorry about your dad. I've learned something here. Vietnam was a dangerous place years ago. But the real danger zone is when someone's heart turns to evil."

Warren nodded. "We're all in trouble when we allow hatred, selfishness, and rebellion to rule our hearts. The war inside men's hearts ultimately is the cause of wars that kill and hurt millions. And Jesus died to change all that."

"Look at how He healed and changed me," Tom said.

Mindy reached out and squeezed Tom's hand. Warren and K.J. stood next to Cheng. A single tear fell from Cheng's eye. But he was still smiling.

Jeff looked up, thinking of Mr. Cao, Mara, Thi Phuong, and Cheng. He realized something about God.

He was smiling too.